W9-ABH-876

CAUSE TO KILL

(AN AVERY BLACK MYSTERY—BOOK 1)

BLAKE PIERCE

ISBN: 978-1-63291-794-2

BOOKS BY BLAKE PIERCE

RILEY PAIGE MYSTERY SERIES
ONCE GONE (Book #1)
ONCE TAKEN (Book #2)
ONCE CRAVED (Book #3)

MACKENZIE WHITE MYSTERY SERIES
BEFORE HE KILLS (Book #1)

AVERY WHITE MYSTERY SERIES
CAUSE TO KILL (Book #1)

PROLOGUE

It was nearly impossible for Cindy Jenkins to leave her sorority's spring party at the Atrium. The massive penthouse space had been fitted with strobe lights, two stocked bars, and a stellar crystal ball that sparkled down on a dance floor packed with partygoers. Throughout the night, she'd danced with no one and everyone. Partners came and went, and Cindy swung her auburn hair and flashed a perfect smile and sky blue stare at any dancer that happened to appear. This was *her* night, a celebration not just for Kappa Kappa Gamma pride, but for the many hard years she'd strived to be the best.

Her future, she knew, was assured.

For the last two years, she'd interned at a major accounting firm in town; they recently offered her a position as a junior accountant. The starting salary would be enough to buy a posh new wardrobe and afford an apartment only a few blocks away from work. Her grades? Top of the class. Sure, she could coast until graduation, but Cindy didn't understand the word "coast." She was all in, every day, no matter what she was doing. Work hard and play hard, that was her motto; and tonight, she wanted to play.

Another cup of the highly alcoholic "Dreamy Blue Slush," another Kappa Kappa Gamma cheer, and another dance, and Cindy couldn't keep the smile off her face. In the strobe lights, she moved in slow motion. Her hair whipped back and her perky nose crinkled at a boy she'd known for years that wanted a kiss. Why not? she thought. Just a peck; nothing serious; nothing to hurt her current relationship, just enough to let everyone at the party know that she wasn't *always* a Type-A goodie-goodie that followed the rules.

Friends spotted her and cheered in approval.

Cindy pulled away from the boy. The dancing and alcohol and heat had finally taken its toll. She swooned slightly, still smiling, and held onto the boy's neck so she wouldn't fall.

"Do you want to go to my house?" he whispered.

"I have a boyfriend."

"Where is he?"

That's right, Cindy thought. Where *is* Winston? He hated sorority parties. *It's just a bunch of stuck-up girls getting drunk and cheating on their boyfriends*, he always said. Well, she thought, I guess I can finally agree! Kissing a boy when she was already committed to another man was probably the raciest thing she'd ever done.

1

You're drunk, she reminded herself. *Get out of here.*

"Gotta go," she slurred.

"One more dance?"

"No," she replied, "really, I've got to go."

The boy begrudgingly accepted her terms. Staring lovingly at the popular Harvard senior, he backed away into the crowd and offered a wave goodbye.

Cindy slid a lock of sweaty hair behind her ear and made her way off the dance floor, eyes low, happiness beaming on her face. Her favorite song came on and she spun and swayed to the edge of the crowd.

"Noooo!" her friends moaned, as they saw her trying to leave.

"Where are you going?" one demanded.

"*Home*," she insisted.

Her best friend, Rachel, pushed through the group and grabbed Cindy's hands. A short, stocky brunette, she wasn't the prettiest or even the smartest of the pack, but her aggressive, sexual nature usually made her the center of attention. She wore a skimpy silver dress, and every time she moved, her body seemed ready to burst out of the garment.

"You *can-not-go!*" she commanded.

"I'm *really* drunk," Cindy pleaded.

"We haven't even played our April Fool's prank! That's the highlight of our party! Please? Just stay a little longer?"

Cindy thought of her boyfriend. They'd been together for two years. That night, they were supposed to have a late-night rendezvous at her apartment. She inwardly groaned at her uncharacteristic dance-floor kiss. How am I supposed to explain *that* one? she wondered.

"*Seriously*," she said, "I *have* to go," and, appealing to Rachel's outrageously erotic nature, she glanced at the boy she'd kissed and humorously added, "If I stay? Who *knows* what could happen?"

"*Oh!*" her friends cheered.

"She is out of control!"

Cindy kissed Rachel on the cheek and whispered, "Have a great night. See you tomorrow," and headed for the door.

Outside, the cool spring air made Cindy take in a deep breath. She wiped the sweat off her face and skipped up Church Street in her short yellow summer dress. The downtown city block was mostly composed of low brick buildings and a few stately houses nestled among trees. A left turn onto Brattle Street and she crossed over and walked southwest.

2

Streetlamps lit most corners, but a section of Brattle Street was blanketed in darkness. Rather than be worried, Cindy picked up her pace and spread her arms wide, as if the shadows could somehow cleanse her system of alcohol and exhaustion and energize her for the rendezvous with Winston.

A narrow alleyway came up on her left. Instinct told her to be careful; it was, after all, extremely late and she wasn't oblivious to the seedier side of Boston, but she was also too high to believe anything could possibly stand in the way of her future.

Out of the corner of her eye, she caught movement, and too late, she turned.

She felt a sudden sharp pain in her neck, one that made her catch her breath, and she glanced back to see something shimmering in the light.

A needle.

Her heart plummeted, and her buzz wore off in a single instant.

At the same moment, she felt someone pressing into her back, a single lean arm trapping hers. The body was smaller than her own, but strong. With a yank, she was pulled backwards into the alley.

"Shhh."

Any thought that it could be a prank vanished the moment she heard the evil, strong voice.

She tried to kick and scream. For some reason, her voice wouldn't work, as if something had softened the muscles in her neck. Her legs, too, began to feel like Jell-O, and she could barely keep her feet on the ground.

Do something! she implored herself, knowing if she didn't she would die.

The arm was around her right-hand side. Cindy turned out of the hold, and at the same time jerked her neck back to head-butt her attacker. The back of her skull smacked into his nose and she could almost hear a "crack." The man swore under his breath and released her.

Run! Cindy pleaded.

But her body refused to comply. Her legs gave out from beneath her, and she fell hard on the cement.

Cindy lay on her back, legs splayed and arms out at opposite angles, unable to move.

The attacker kneeled down beside her. His face was obscured by a sloppily placed wig, a fake moustache, and thick glasses. The eyes behind the glasses sent a chill through her body: cold and hard. Soulless.

3

"I love you," he said.

Cindy tried to scream; a gurgle came out.

The man nearly touched her face; then, as if aware of their surroundings, he quickly stood.

Cindy felt herself gripped by the hands and pulled through the alley.

Her eyes filled with tears.

Someone, she mentally pleaded, *help me. Help!* She remembered her classmates, her friends, her laughter at the party. *Help!*

At the end of the path, the small man lifted her up and hugged her tight. Her head flopped on his shoulder. He lovingly stroked her hair.

He grabbed one of her hands and twirled her around like they were lovers.

"It's all right," he said loudly, as if it were meant for others, "I'll get the door."

Cindy spotted people farther off in the distance. Thinking was difficult. Nothing would move; an effort to speak failed.

The passenger side of a blue minivan was opened. He plopped her inside and carefully closed the door so that her head rested on the window.

On the driver's side, he entered and placed a soft, pillow-like sack over her head.

"Sleep, my love," she said, turning the ignition. "Sleep."

The van pulled away, and as Cindy's mind faded into darkness, her final thought was of her future, her bright, unbelievable future that had suddenly, horribly been snatched away.

CHAPTER ONE

Avery Black stood in the back of the packed conference room, leaning into a wall, deep in thought as she took in the proceedings around her. Over thirty officers packed the small conference room of the Boston Police Department on New Sudbury Street. Two walls were painted yellow; two were glass and looked out upon the department's second floor. Captain Mike O'Malley, early fifties, a small, powerfully built Boston native with dark eyes and hair, kept moving around behind the podium. He seemed to Avery to be perpetually restless, uncomfortable in his own skin.

"Last but not least," he said in his thick accent, "I'd like to welcome Avery Black to Homicide Squad."

A few perfunctory claps filled the room, which otherwise remained embarrassingly silent.

"*Now, now*," the captain snapped, "that's no way to treat a new detective. Black had more arrests than any of you last year, and she nearly singlehandedly took down the West Side Killers. Give her some respect," he said and nodded toward the back with a noncommittal smile.

Head low, Avery knew her bleached-blond hair hid her features. Dressed more like an attorney than a cop, in her sharp black pantsuit and button-down shirt, her attire, a throwback from her days as a defense lawyer, was yet another reason that most within the police department chose to either shun her or to curse her name behind her back.

"Avery!" The captain raised his arms. "I'm trying to give you some props over here. Wake up!"

She looked around, flustered, at the sea of hostile faces staring back. She was starting to wonder whether coming to Homicide was a good idea after all.

"All right, let's start the day," the captain added to the rest of the room. "Avery, you, in my office. *Now*." He turned to another cop. "And I want to see you too, and you, Hennessey, get over here. And Charlie, why you running out of here so fast?"

Avery waited for the throng of police officers to leave, then as she began to make her way toward his office, a cop stood in front of her, one she had seen around the department but had never formally greeted. Ramirez was slightly taller than her, lean and sophisticated in appearance, with tan Latin skin. He had short black hair, a shaved face, and although he wore a nice gray suit, there was an ease about his stance and appearance. A sip of coffee and he continued to stare without emotion.

"Can I help you?" she asked.

"It's the other way around," he said. "I'm the one that's going to help you."

He offered a hand; she didn't take it.

"Just trying to get a bead on the infamous Avery Black. Lot of rumors. Wanted to figure out which ones were true. So far I've got: absentminded, acts like she's too good for the force. Check and check. Two for two. Not bad for a Monday."

Abuse within the police force was nothing new for Avery. It had started three years ago when she entered as a rookie cop, and it hadn't let up since. Few in the department were considered friends, and even fewer trusted colleagues.

Avery brushed past him.

"Good luck with the chief," Ramirez sarcastically called out, "I hear he can be a real asshole."

A limp, backhanded wave was offered in reply. Over the years, Avery had learned it was better to acknowledge her hostile partners than avoid them completely, just to let them know she was there and wasn't going away.

The second floor of the A1 police department in central Boston was an expansive, churning engine of activity. Cubicles filled the center of the expansive workspace, and smaller glass offices surrounded the side windows. Cops glared at Avery as she passed.

"Murderer," someone muttered under his breath.

"Homicide will be perfect for you," said another.

Avery passed a female Irish cop whom she had saved from the clutches of a gang den; she flashed Avery a quick glance and whispered, "Good luck, Avery. You deserve it."

Avery smiled. "Thanks."

Her first kind word of the day gave her a boost of confidence that she took with her into the captain's office. To her surprise, Ramirez stood only a few feet outside the glass partition. He lifted his coffee and grinned.

"Come on in," the captain said. "And close the door behind you."

Avery sat down.

O'Malley was even more formidable close up. The dye job on his hair was noticeable, along with the many wrinkles around his eyes and mouth. He rubbed his temples and sat back.

"You like it here?" he asked.

6

"What do you mean?"

"I mean this, the A1. Heart of Boston. You're in the thick of it, here. Big City Dog. You're a small-town girl, right? Oklahoma?"

"Ohio."

"Right, right," he muttered. "What is it about the A1 you like so much? There are a lot of other departments in Boston. You could have started at Southside, B2, maybe D14 and got a taste of the suburbs. Lots of gangs out there. You only applied here."

"I like big cities."

"We get some real sickos here. You sure you wanna go down that road again? This is homicide. A little different than beat."

"I watched the leader of the West Side Killers flay someone alive while the rest of his gang sang songs and watched. What kind of 'sickos' are we talking about?"

O'Malley watched her every move.

"The way I hear it," he said, "you got played—hard—by that Harvard psycho. He made you look like a fool. Destroyed your life. From star attorney to disgraced attorney, then nothing. And then the switch to rookie cop. That had to hurt."

Avery squirmed in her chair. Why did he have to rehash all this? Why now? Today was a day to celebrate her promotion to Homicide, and she didn't want to ruin it—and certainly didn't want to dwell on the past. What was done was done. She could only look forward.

"You turned it around, though"—he nodded in respect—"made a new life for yourself down here. On the right side this time. Gotta respect that. But," he said, looking her over, "I want to make sure you're ready. Are you ready?"

She stared back, wondering where he was going with this.

"If I wasn't ready," she said, "I wouldn't be here."

He nodded, seemingly satisfied.

"We just got a call," he said. "A dead girl. *Staged.* It doesn't look good. Guys on the scene don't know what to make of it."

Avery's heart beat faster.

"I'm ready," she said.

"Are you?" he asked. "You're good, but if this turns out to be something big, I want to make sure you won't crack."

"I don't crack," she said.

"That's what I wanted to hear," he said and pushed some papers on his desk. "Dylan Connelly supervises Homicide. He's over there now working with forensics. You've got a new partner, too. Try not to get him killed."

7

"That wasn't my fault," Avery complained, and she inwardly bristled at the recent Internal Affairs investigation, all because her former partner—a prejudiced hothead—had jumped the gun and tried to infiltrate a gang all by himself and take credit for her work.

The chief pointed outside.

"Your partner's waiting. I've made you lead detective. Don't let me down."

She turned to see Ramirez waiting. She groaned.

"Ramirez? Why him?"

"Honestly?" The captain shrugged. "He's the only one that wanted to work with you. Everyone else here seems to hate you."

She felt that knot in her stomach tightening.

"Tread softly, young detective," he added, as he stood, signaling their meeting was over. "You need all the friends you can get."

CHAPTER TWO

"How did it go?" Ramirez asked, as Avery exited the office.

She lowered her head and kept on walking. Avery hated small talk, and she didn't trust any of her fellow cops to talk to her without trading barbs.

"Where are we headed?" she replied.

"All business." Ramirez smiled. "Good to know. All right, Black; we've got a dead girl placed on a bench in Lederman Park, by the river. It's a high-traffic area. Not really a place you'd put a body."

Officers slapped palms with Ramirez.

"Go get her, tiger!"

"Break her in right, Ramirez."

Avery shook her head. "Nice," she said.

Ramirez raised his hands.

"It's not me."

"It's all of you," she sneered. "I never thought a police station would be worse than a law firm. Secret boys' club, right? No girls allowed?"

"Easy, Black."

She headed toward the elevators. A few officers cheered at getting under her skin. Usually, Avery was able to ignore it, but something about her new case had already shaken her tough exterior. The words the captain had used weren't typical of a simple homicide: *Don't know what to make of it. Staged.*

And the cocky, aloof air of her new partner wasn't exactly comforting: *Seems cut and dry.* Nothing was ever cut and dry.

The elevator door was about to close when Ramirez put his hand through.

"I'm sorry, all right?"

He seemed sincere. Palms up, an apologetic look in his dark eyes. A button was pressed and they moved down.

Avery glanced at him.

"The captain said you were the only one that wanted to work with me. Why?"

"You're Avery Black," he replied as if the answer were obvious. "How could I not be curious? Nobody really knows you, but everyone seems to have an opinion: idiot, genius, has-been, up-and-comer, murderer, savior. I wanted to sort out fact from fiction."

"Why do *you* care?"

Ramirez flashed an enigmatic smile.

9

But he said nothing.

* * *

Avery followed Ramirez as he walked easily through the parking garage. He wore no tie and his top two buttons were open.

"I'm over there," he pointed.

They passed a few uniformed officers that seemed to know him; one waved and flashed a strange look that seemed to ask: *What are you doing with her?*

He led her to a dusty, crimson Cadillac, old, with torn tan seats on the inside.

"Solid ride," Avery joked.

"This baby has saved me many times," he relayed with pride as he lovingly pat the hood. "All I have to do is dress like a pimp or a starving Spaniard and nobody pays me any mind."

They headed out of the lot.

Lederman Park was only a few miles from the police station. They drove west on Cambridge Street and took a right on Blossom.

"So," Ramirez said, "I heard you were a lawyer once."

"Yeah?" Guarded blue eyes flashed him a sidelong glance. "What else did you hear?"

"Criminal defense attorney," he added, "best of the best. You worked at Goldfinch & Seymour. Not a shabby operation. What made you quit?"

"You don't know?"

"I know you defended a lot of scumbags. Perfect record, right? You even had a few dirty cops put behind bars. Must have been living the life. Huge salary, an endless stream of success. What kind of person leaves all that behind to join the force?"

Avery remembered the house she'd grown up in, a small farm surrounded by flat land for miles. The solitude had never suited her. Neither had the animals or the smell of the place: feces and fur and feathers. From the beginning she'd wanted to get out. She had: Boston. First the university and then the law school and career.

And now this.

A sigh escaped her lips.

"I guess, sometimes things don't work out the way we plan."

"What's that supposed to mean?"

In her mind, she saw the smile again, that old, sinister smile from a wrinkled old man with thick glasses. He'd seemed so sincere at first, so humble and smart and honest. *All* of them had, she realized.

Until their trials were over and they went back to their everyday lives and she was forced to accept that she was no savior of the helpless, no defender of the people, but a pawn, a simple pawn in a game too complex and rooted to change.

"Life is hard," she mused. "You think you know something one day and then the next day, the veil gets pulled down and everything changes."

He nodded.

"Howard Randall," he said, clearly realizing.

The name made her more aware of everything—the cool air in the car, her position on the seat, their location in the city. Nobody had said his name aloud in a long time, especially to her. She felt exposed and vulnerable, and in response she tightened her body and sat taller.

"Sorry," he said, "I didn't mean to—"

"It's fine," she said.

Only it wasn't fine. Everything had ended after him. Her life. Her job. Her sanity. Being a defense attorney had been challenging, to say the least, but *he* was the one that was supposed to make it right again. A genius Harvard professor, respected by all, simple and kind, he'd been charged with murder. Avery's salvation was supposed to come through *his* defense. For once, she was supposed to do what she had dreamed about since childhood: defend the *innocent* and ensure justice prevailed.

But nothing like that happened.

11

CHAPTER THREE

The park had already been closed off to the public.

Two plainclothes officers flagged down Ramirez's car and quickly waved them away from the main parking lot and over to the left. Among the officers that were obviously from her department, Avery spotted a number of state police.

"Why are the troopers here?" she asked.

"Their home base is right up the street."

Ramirez pulled over and parked next to a line of police cruisers. Yellow tape had sectioned off a large area of the lot. News vans, reporters, cameras, and a bunch of other runners and park regulars stood by the tape to try to see what was happening.

"Nobody beyond this point," an officer said.

Avery flashed a badge.

"Homicide," she said. It was the first time she'd actually acknowledged her new position, and it filled her with pride.

"Where's Connelly?" Ramirez asked.

An officer pointed toward the trees.

They made their way across the grass, a baseball diamond on their left. More yellow tape met them before a line of trees. Under thick foliage was a walking path that wound its way along the Charles River. A single officer, along with a forensics specialist and a photographer, stood before a bench.

Avery avoided initial contact with those already on the scene. Over the years, she'd come to find that social interactions strained her focus, and too many questions and formalities with others sullied her point of view. Sadly, it was yet another characteristic of hers that had incurred the scorn of her entire department.

The victim was a young girl placed askew on the bench. She was obviously dead, but with the exception of her bluish skin tone, her position and facial expression might have made the average passerby think twice before they wondered if something was wrong.

Like a lover waiting for her paramour, the girl's hands were placed on the bench-back. Her chin rested on her hands. A mischievous smile curled on her lips. Her body was turned, as if she'd been in a sitting position and had moved to look for someone or breathe out a heavy sigh. She was clothed in a yellow summer dress and white flip-flops, lovely auburn hair flowing over her left shoulder. Her legs were crossed and her toes rested gently on the path.

Only the victim's eyes gave away her torment. They emanated the pain and disbelief.

Avery heard a voice in her mind, the voice of the old man that haunted her nights and daydreams. In regards to his own victims, he had once asked her: *What are they? Only vessels, nameless, faceless vessels—so few among billions—waiting to find their purpose.*

Anger rose up in her, anger born at being exposed and humiliated and most of all, from having her entire life shattered.

She moved closer to the body.

As an attorney, she'd been forced to examine endless forensics reports and coroner's photos and anything else related to her case. Her education had vastly improved as a cop, when she routinely analyzed murder victims in person, and could make more honest assessments.

The dress, she noticed, had been washed, and the victim's hair cleaned. The nails and toenails were freshly polished, and when she took a deep whiff of skin, she smelled coconut and honey and only the faint hint of formaldehyde.

"You gonna kiss it or what?" someone said.

Avery was bent over the victim's body, hands behind her back. On the bench was a yellow placard labeled "4." Beside it, on the girl's lower waist, was a stiff orange hair, barely perceptible among the yellow of her dress.

Homicide Supervisor Dylan Connelly stood akimbo and waited for an answer. He was tough and rugged, with wavy blond hair and penetrating blue eyes. His chest and arms nearly tore out of his blue shirt. His pants were brown linen, and thick black boots adorned his feet. Avery had noticed him often in the office; he wasn't exactly her type, but he had an animal ferocity about him that she admired.

"This is a crime scene, Black. Next time, watch where you're walking. You're lucky we already dusted for prints and shoes."

She looked down, baffled; she had been careful where she had walked. She looked up at Connelly's steely eyes and realized he was just looking for a reason to ride her.

"I didn't know it was a crime scene," she said. "Thanks for filling me in."

Ramirez snickered.

Connelly bit down and stepped forward.

"You know why people can't stand you, Black? It's not just that you're an outsider, it's that *when* you were on the outside, you had no real respect for cops, and now that you're on the inside, you have even less respect. Let me be perfectly clear: I don't like you, I don't trust you, and I sure as hell didn't want you on my team."

He turned to Ramirez.

"Fill her in on what we know. I'm going home to take a shower. I feel sick," he said. Gloves were removed and thrown to the ground. To Avery, he added: "I expect a full report by the end of the day. Five o'clock sharp. Conference room. You hear me? Don't be late. And make sure you clean this mess up, too, before you leave. State troopers were kind enough to step aside and let us work. *You* be kind enough and show them some courtesy."

Connelly walked away in a huff.

"You have a real way with people," Ramirez admired.

Avery shrugged.

The forensics specialist on the scene was a shapely young African American named Randy Johnson. She had large eyes and an easy way about herself. Short, dreadlocked hair was only partially hidden behind a white cap.

Avery had worked with her before. They'd formed a fast bond during a domestic violence case. The last time they'd seen each other was over drinks.

Excited to be on another case with Avery, Randy held out a hand, noticed her own glove, blushed, guffawed, and said, "Oops," followed by a wacky, *eek!* expression and the proclamation: "I might be *contaminated*."

"Good to see you too, Randy."

"Congrats on Homicide." Randy bowed. "Moving up in the world."

"One wacko at a time. What have we got?"

"I'd say someone was in love," Randy replied. "Cleaned her up pretty good. Opened her up from the back. Drained her body, filled her up so she wouldn't rot, and stitched her up again. Fresh clothes. Manicure. Careful too. No prints yet. Not much to go on until I get to the lab. Only two wounds I can find. See the mouth? You can either pin this from the inside, or use gel to get a corpse to smile like that. From the puncture wound here," she pointed at the corner of a lip, "I'd guess injection. There's another one here," she noted on the neck. "By the coloring, this came earlier, maybe at the time of abduction. Body has been dead for about forty-eight hours. Found a couple of interesting hairs."

"How long has she been here?"

"Bikers found her at six," Ramirez said. "The park is patrolled every night around midnight and three a.m. They didn't see anything."

Avery couldn't stop staring at the dead girl's eyes. They seemed to be looking at something in the distance, yet close to the shoreline, on their side of the river. She carefully maneuvered to the back of the bench and tried to follow the line of sight. Downriver, there were a bunch of low brick buildings; one of them was short; a white dome rested on its on top.

"What building is that?" she asked. "The large one with the dome?"

Ramirez squinted.

"Maybe the Omni Theatre?"

"Can we find out what's playing?"

"Why?"

"I don't know, just a hunch."

Avery stood up.

"Do we know who she is?"

"Yeah," Ramirez replied and checked his notes. "We think her name is Cindy Jenkins. Harvard senior. Sorority sister. Kappa Kappa Gamma. Went missing two nights ago. Campus police and Cambridge cops put her picture up last night. Connelly had his people check through photos. Hers was a match. We still need confirmation. I'll call the family."

"How are we on surveillance?"

"Jones and Thompson are on that now. You know them, right? Great detectives. They're assigned to us for the day. After that, we're on our own unless we can prove we need the extra resources. No entrance cameras to the park, but there are some up the highway and across the street. We should know something this afternoon."

"Any witnesses?"

"None so far. The bikers are clean. I can troll around."

Avery surveyed the surrounding area. Yellow tape encompassed a large swath of the park. Nothing out of the ordinary could be found near the river or on the bike path or grass. She tried to form a mental picture of events. He would have driven in through the main road, parked his car close to the water for easy access to the bench. How did he get the body to the bench without causing suspicion?

She wondered. People might have been watching. He had to prepare for that. Maybe he made it look like she was alive? Avery turned back to the body. It was a definite possibility. The girl was

15

beautiful, even in death, ethereal almost. He had obviously spent a lot of time and planning to ensure she looked perfect. Not a gang kill, she realized. Not a scorned lover. This was different. Avery had seen it before.

Suddenly, she wondered if O'Malley was right. Maybe she *wasn't* ready.

"Can I borrow your car?" she asked.

Ramirez cocked a brow.

"What about the crime scene?"

She offered a confident shrug.

"You're a big boy. Figure it out."

"Where are *you* going?"

"Harvard."

CHAPTER FOUR

He sat in an office cubicle—superior, victorious, more powerful than anyone on the planet. A computer screen was open before him. With a deep breath, he closed his eyes, and remembered.

He recalled the cavernous basement of his home, more like a garden nursery. Multiple varieties of poppy flowers lined the main room: red, yellow, and white. Many other psychedelic plants—each one accrued over countless years—had been placed in long troughs; some were alien-like weeds or intriguing flowers; many had a more common appearance that would have been overlooked in any wildlife setting, despite their potent abilities. A timed watering system, temperature gauge, and LED lights kept them thriving.

A long hallway made of wooden beams led to other rooms. On the walls were pictures. Most of the pictures were of animals in various stages of death, and then "rebirth" as they were stuffed and positioned: a tabby cat on its hind legs playing with yarn; a white and black spotted dog, rolled over and waiting for a tummy rub.

Doors came next. He imagined the door on the left opened. There, he saw her again, her naked body laid out on a silver table. Strong fluorescent lighting lit the space. In a glass case were many colorful liquids in clear jars.

He'd felt her skin when he'd rubbed his fingers along the outside of her thigh. Mentally, he reenacted each delicate procedure: her body drained, preserved, cleaned, and stuffed. Throughout the rebirth, he took photos that would later cover more walls saved for his human trophies. Some of the photos had already been placed.

Tremendous, surreal energy flowed through him.

For years, he had avoided humans. They were scary, more violent and uncontrollable than animals. He loved animals. Humans, however, he discovered to be more potent sacrifices for the All Spirit. After the girl's death, he'd seen the sky open, and the shadowy image of the Great Creator had looked at him and said: *More.*

His reverie was broken by a snapping voice.

"You daydreaming again?"

A grumbling worker stood overhead with a scowl on his face. He had the face and body of a former football player. A sharp blue suit did little to diminish his ferocity.

17

Meekly, he lowered his head. His shoulders slightly hunched, and he transformed into a forgettable, diminutive worker.

"I'm sorry, Mr. Peet."

"I'm tired of the apologies. Get me those figures."

Inwardly, the killer smiled like a laughing giant. At work, the game was almost as exciting as his private life. No one knew how *special* he was, how dedicated and *essential* to the delicate balance of the universe. None of them would receive an honored place in the realm of the Overworld. Their everyday, mundane, earthly tasks: dressing up, having meetings, pushing money around from place to place—were meaningless; it was only meaningful to him because it connected him to the outside world and allowed him to do the Lord's work.

His boss grumbled and walked away.

Eyes still closed, the killer imagined his Overlord: the shadowy, dark figure that whispered in his dreams and directed his thoughts.

A song of homage formed on his lips, and he sang in a whisper: "Oh Lord, oh Lord, our work is pure. Ask and I give you: More."

More.

CHAPTER FIVE

Avery had a name: Cindy Jenkins. She knew the sorority: Kappa Kappa Gamma. And she was fully aware of Harvard University. The ivy league school had rejected her as an incoming freshman, but she'd still found a way to soak in Harvard life throughout her own college career, as she'd dated two boys from the school.

Unlike other colleges, the sororities and fraternities of Harvard weren't officially acknowledged. No Greek houses existed on or off campus. Partying, however, happened regularly at multiple off-campus houses or apartment complexes under the name of "organizations" or specialized "clubs." Avery had witnessed firsthand the paradox of college life during her own college tenure. Everyone pretended to be solely focused on grades until the sun went down and they transformed into a bunch of wild, partying animals.

At a red light, Avery performed a quick Internet search to discover that Kappa Kappa Gamma rented two areas on the same block in Cambridge: Church Street. One of the locations was for events, the other for meetings and socializing.

She drove over Longfellow Bridge, past MIT, and hung a right onto Massachusetts Avenue. Harvard Yard appeared on her right with its magnificent red brick buildings set among a forest of trees and paved pathways.

A parking spot opened on Church Street.

Avery parked, locked the car door, and lifted her face to the sun. It was a warm day, with temperatures in the high seventies. She checked the time: ten thirty.

The Kappa building was a long, two-story structure with a brick facade. The first floor housed a number of clothing shops. The second floor, Avery guessed, was reserved for office space and sorority operations. The only designation next to the second-floor buzzer was the blue fleur-de-lis symbol of Harvard; she pressed it.

A scratchy female voice came on the intercom system.

"Yeah?"

"Police," she growled, "open up."

Silence for a moment.

"Seriously," the voice replied, "who is this?"

"It's the police," she said in earnest. "Everything is fine. No one is in trouble. I just need to speak with someone in Kappa Kappa Gamma."

The door buzzed open.

At the top of the steps, Avery was greeted by a sleepy, haggard girl in an oversized gray sweatshirt and white sweatpants. Dark-haired, she appeared hard-partying. Wisps of hair hid most of her face. There were dark circles under her eyes, and the body that she normally took so much pride in accentuating appeared thick and formless.

"What do you want?" she asked.

"Calm down," Avery offered. "This has nothing to do with sorority activities. I'm just here to ask a few questions."

"Can I see some identification?"

Avery flashed her badge.

She sized up Avery, inspected the badge, and stood back.

The space for Kappa Kappa Gamma was large and bright. The ceiling was high. A number of comfortable tan couches and blue bean bags littered the area. Walls had been painted dark blue. There was a bar, a sound system, and a huge, flat-screen TV. The windows were nearly floor to ceiling. Across the street, Avery could see the top of another short apartment complex, and then the sky. A few clouds rolled by.

She guessed her college experience was a lot different from that of most of the girls in Kappa Kappa Gamma. For one, she had paid for school herself. Every day after classes she went to a local law firm and worked her way up from a secretary to an honored paralegal. She also rarely drank in school. Her father had been a raging alcoholic. Most college nights, she was either the designated driver or in the dorm studying.

A burst of hope flashed on the girl's face.

"Is this about Cindy?" she asked.

"Is Cindy a friend of yours?"

"Yeah, my *best* friend," she said. "Please, tell me she's all right?"

"What's your name?"

"Rachel Strauss."

"Are you the one that called the police?"

"That's right. Cindy left our party pretty drunk on Saturday night. No one has seen her since. That's not like her." She rolled her eyes and offered a slight smile when she added, "She's usually very predictable. She's just like, Ms. Perfect, you know? Always to bed

20

at the same time, same schedule that never changes—needs like, five years' notice for any changes. Saturday she was crazy. Drinking. Dancing. Threw the clock away for a while. It was nice to see."

A distant gaze took Rachel for a moment.

"She was just, really happy, you know?"

"Any particular reason?" Avery wondered.

"I don't know, top of her class. Has a job lined up for the fall."

"What job?"

"Devante? They're like, the *best* firm in Boston. She was an accounting major. So boring, I know, but she was a genius when it came to numbers."

"Can you tell me about Saturday night?"

Tears came to Rachel's eyes.

"This *is* about Cindy, isn't it?"

"Yeah," Avery said. "Maybe we can sit down?"

Rachel crashed on the couch and cried.

Through sobs, she tried to speak.

"Is she all right? Where is she?"

It was the part of the job Avery hated the most—talking to relatives and friends. There was only so much she was allowed to discuss. The more people learned about a case, the more they talked, and that talk had a way of getting back to the perpetrators of crimes. No one ever understood that or cared in the moment: they were too distressed. All they wanted were answers.

Avery sat beside her.

"We're really glad you called," she said. "You did the right thing. I'm afraid I can't talk about an ongoing investigation. What I *can* tell you is that I'm doing everything in my power to find out what happened to Cindy that night. I can't do it alone, I need your help."

Rachel nodded and wiped her eyes.

"I can help," she said, "I can help."

"I'd like to know everything you remember about that night, and Cindy. Who was she talking to? Was there anything that stood out in your mind? Comments she made? People that took an interest in her? Anything about when she left?"

Rachel broke down completely.

Eventually, she raised a hand and nodded and pulled herself together.

"Yeah," she said, "sure."

21

"Where is everyone else?" Avery asked as a distraction. "I thought sorority houses were supposed to be packed with hungover girls in Kappa gear."

"They're at class," Rachel said and wiped her eyes. "A couple of girls went out to get breakfast. By the way," she added, "we're not technically a sorority house. This is just a place we rent to crash when we don't want to go back to our dorm. Cindy never stayed here. Too modern for her. She has more of a 'homey' air."

"Where does she live?"

"Student housing not far from here," Rachel said. "But she wasn't headed home on Saturday night. She was supposed to meet up with her boyfriend."

Avery's senses heightened.

"Boyfriend?"

Rachel nodded.

"Winston Graves, big-time senior, rower, asshole. None of us ever understood why she dated him. Well, I guess I did. He's handsome and comes from tons of money. Cindy never had any money. I think, when you don't come from money, it's really appealing."

Yeah, Avery thought, I know. She remembered how the money and prestige and power of her previous law firm job had made her believe she was somehow different from that scared and determined young girl who had left Ohio.

"Where does Winston live?" she asked.

"In Winthrop Square. It's really close to here. But Cindy never made it. Winston came over early on Sunday morning looking for her. He assumed she'd just forgotten about their plans and passed out. So we went to her house together. She wasn't there, either. That's when I called the police."

"Would she have gone anywhere else?"

"No way," Rachel said. "That's not like Cindy at all."

"So when she left here, you're sure she was headed over to Winston's house."

"Absolutely."

"Was there anything that might have changed those plans? Anything that happened to her early in the evening, or even at the end?"

Rachel shook her head.

"No, well," she realized, "there was *something*. I'm sure it's nothing, but there's this boy that's had a crush on Cindy for years. His name is George Fine. He's handsome, tough-looking, a loner,

22

but a little weird, if you know what I mean? Works out and jogs around campus a lot. I had a class with him once last year. One of our jokes was that he's been in a class with Cindy nearly every semester since freshman year. He's been obsessed with her. He was here Saturday, and the crazy thing is, Cindy was dancing with him, and they even kissed. Totally not like Cindy. I mean, she's dating Winston—not that they have the perfect relationship—but she was really drunk, and raging. They kissed, danced, and then she left."

"Did George follow her out?"

"I don't know," she said. "Honestly. I don't remember seeing him after Cindy left, but that might be because I was totally wasted."

"Do you remember what time she left?"

"Yeah," she said, "at exactly two forty-five. Saturday was our annual April Fool's Night party, and we're supposed to play this great joke, but everyone was having so much fun we forgot about it until Cindy left."

Rachel lowered her head. Emptiness filled the air for a while.

"Well look," Avery said, "this has been really helpful. Thank you. Here's my card. If you can remember anything else, or if your sorority sisters have something to add, I'd love to hear about it. This is an open investigation, so even the smallest detail might give us a lead."

Rachel faced her then with tears in her eyes. And as the tears began to roll down her cheeks, her voice remained calm and steady.

"She's dead," she said, "isn't she?"

"Rachel, I can't."

Rachel nodded, and then she cupped her face in her hands and completely broke down. Avery leaned over and hugged her tight.

23

CHAPTER SIX

Outside, Avery turned her face to the sun and breathed out a heavy sigh.

Church Street was busy, and there were numerous storefront cameras. Even in the middle of the night, she couldn't believe it was where the abduction had taken place.

Where did you go? she wondered.

A quick check on her phone revealed the easiest route to Winthrop Square. She took a stroll up Church and turned left on Brattle. Brattle Street was wider than Church, with just as many shops. Across the street, she noticed the Brattle Theatre. A small alley was on one side of the building, buttressed by a coffee house. Trees hid the area in shadows. Curious, Avery crossed over and entered the narrow strip between buildings.

She moved out onto Brattle again and checked every storefront within a one-block radius on both sides of Church Street. There were at least two stores with cameras outside.

She headed into a small smoke shop.

The bell on the door clanged.

"Can I help you?" said an old, white hippie with dreadlocked hair.

"Yeah," Avery said, "I notice you have a camera out front. What kind of range do you get on that thing?"

"The whole block," he said, "both directions. Had to install it two years ago. Goddamn college students. Everyone thinks these Harvard kids are so special, but they're just a bunch of assholes like everyone else. For years they've been smashing my windows. Some kind of college prank, right? Not for me. You know how much those windows cost?"

"Sorry to hear that. Listen, I don't have a warrant," she said and flashed her badge, "but some of those idiot kids might have caused a disturbance right up your street. No cameras there. Any way I can take a look? I know the time. Shouldn't take too long."

He frowned and mumbled to himself.

"I don't know," he said, "I've got to watch the shop. I'm the only one here."

"I'll make it worth your while." She smiled. "How about fifty bucks."

Without a word, he lowered his head, walked around the counter, and turned the sign on the door from "open" to "closed."

24

"Fifty bucks?" he said. "Come on in!"

The back of the shop was cluttered and dark. Hidden among boxes and spare supplies, the man uncovered a small television set. Above the set—on a higher shelf—was a series of electronic equipment attached to the TV.

"Don't really use it that often," he said, "only when there's trouble. Tapes get erased every week on Monday night. When was your little incident?"

"Saturday night," she said.

"All right, then, you're in luck."

He turned on the set.

The black-and-white image was from right outside the shop. Avery could clearly see the entrance to the store, as well as the opposite side of the street and right up Brattle. The area she specifically wanted to investigate was about fifty yards away. The image was grainier, and it was nearly impossible to make out shapes in front of the alley.

A small mouse was used to scan backwards.

"What time did you say?" he asked.

"Two forty-five," she said, "but I'll need to check some other times as well. Do you mind if I just sit down and look for myself? You can get back to the shop."

A suspicious brow greeted her.

"Are you going to steal anything?"

"I'm a cop," she said. "That goes against my motto."

"Then you're not like any cop *I* know," he laughed.

Avery pulled out a small black chair. She wiped off the dust and took a seat. A quick review of the equipment and she was able to easily scan forward and back.

At two forty-five, a few people walked up and down Brattle Street.

At two fifty, the street appeared empty.

By two-fifty two, someone—a girl by the hair and dress—came into view from the direction of Church. She walked across Brattle and turned left. Once she passed the coffee shop, a dark image from under the trees merged with hers, and they both disappeared. For a moment, Avery could only see the indecipherable motion of various shades of black. As the scene continued, the tree shapes took on their original form. The girl never reappeared.

"Shit," Avery whispered.

She unclipped a sleek, modern walkie-talkie from the back of her belt.

25

"Ramirez," she said. "Where are you?"

"Who is this?" came a crackling voice.

"You know who this is. Your new partner."

"I'm still at Lederman. Almost finished here. They just took away the body."

"I need you down here, now," she said and gave him the location. "I think I know where Cindy Jenkins was abducted."

* * *

An hour later, Avery had the alleyway blocked off on both sides by yellow tape. On Brattle Street, a police car and the forensics van were pulled up onto the sidewalk. One officer had been stationed to discourage visitors.

The alley opened into a wide, darkened street about halfway into the block. One side of the street housed a glass real estate building and a loading dock. On the other side were housing complexes. There was a parking lot that could support four cars. Another police car, along with more yellow tape, was at the end of the alley.

Avery stood in front of the loading dock.

"There," she said and pointed to a high camera. "We need that footage. It probably belongs to the real estate company. Let's get in there and see what we can find."

Ramirez shook his head.

"You're crazy," he said. "That tape didn't show shit."

"Cindy Jenkins had no reason to walk down this alley," Avery said. "Her boyfriend lives in the opposite direction."

"Maybe she wanted to go for a walk," he argued. "All I'm saying is, this is a lot of manpower for a hunch."

"It's no hunch. You saw the tape."

"I saw a bunch of black blurs I couldn't understand!" He fought. "Why would the killer attack here? There are cameras everywhere. He'd have to be a complete idiot."

"Let's go find out," she said.

Top Real Estate Company owned the glass building and the loading dock.

After a brief discussion with front desk security, Avery and Ramirez were told to wait on the plush leather couches for someone of higher authority to arrive. Ten minutes later, the head of security and the president of the company appeared.

Avery flashed her best smile and shook hands.

"Thanks for seeing us," she said. "We'd like to access the camera right above your loading dock. We don't have a warrant," she frowned, "but what we do have is a dead girl that was abducted on Saturday night, most likely right outside your back door. Unless something comes up, we should be in and out in twenty minutes."

"And if something comes up?" the president asked.

"Then you made the right choice to assist the police in an extremely timely and delicate matter. A warrant could take an entire day. The body of that girl has already been dead for two days. She can't talk anymore. She can't help us. But you can. Please help. Every second we waste, the trail gets cold."

The president nodded to himself and turned to his guard.

"Davis," he said, "show them up. Give them whatever they need. If there are any problems," he said to Avery, "please come and find me."

When they were on their way, Ramirez whistled to himself.

"What a charmer," he said.

"Whatever it takes," Avery whispered.

The security office at Top Real Estate was a buzzing room filled with over twenty television screens. The guard sat down at the black table and keyboard.

"OK," he said. "Time and place?"

"Loading dock. About two fifty-two and then let's move forward."

Ramirez shook his head.

"We're not going to find nothing."

The real estate cameras were of a much higher quality than the smoke shop, and in color. Most of the viewing screens were of a similar size, but one in particular was large. The guard put the loading-dock camera on the larger screen and then spun the image backwards.

"There," Avery called. "Stop."

The image halted at two-fifty. The camera showed a panoramic view of the parking lot directly across from the loading dock, as well as left, toward the dead-end sign and the street beyond. There was only a partial view of the alley that led toward Brattle. A single car was parked in the lot: a minivan that appeared to be dark blue.

"That car's not supposed to be there," the guard pointed.

"Can you make out the license?" Avery wondered.

"Yeah, I got it," Ramirez said.

All three of them waited. For a while, the only motion came from cars on the perpendicular street, and the motion from trees.

At two-fifty-three, two people came into view.

They might have been lovers.

One was a smaller man, wiry and short, with thick, bushy hair, a moustache, and glasses. The other was a girl, taller with long hair. She wore a light summer dress and sandals. They appeared to be dancing. He held one of her hands and spun her around from the waist.

"Holy shit," Ramirez said, "that's Jenkins."

"Same dress," Avery said, "shoes, hair."

"She's drugged," he said. "Look at her. Feet are dragging."

They watched the killer open the passenger door and place her inside. Then, as he turned and walked around to the driver's side, he looked directly into the loading-dock camera, bowed in a theatrical way, and twirled to the driver's side door.

"Holy *shit*!" Ramirez howled. "Motherfucker is playing with us."

"I want everyone on this," Avery said. "Thompson and Jones are full-time surveillance from now on. Thompson can stay at the park. Tell him about the minivan. That will narrow down his search. We need to know what direction that car was heading. Jones has a harder job. He needs to get over here now and follow that van. I don't care how he does it. Tell him to track down any cameras that can help him along the way."

She turned to Ramirez, who stared back, shocked and impressed.

"We've got our killer."

CHAPTER SEVEN

Exhaustion finally hit Avery at close to six forty-five in the evening, on the elevator ride up to the second floor of the police station. All the energy and impetus she'd received from the morning revelations had culminated in a day well spent, but a night with countless unanswered questions. Her light skin was partially burned from the sun, her hair a mess, the jacket she'd worn earlier strung over her arm. Her shirt: dirty and untucked. Ramirez, on the other hand, appeared even more refreshed than he had in the morning: hair slicked back, suit almost perfectly pressed, eyes sharp and only a dab of sweat on his forehead.

"How can you possibly look so good?" she asked.

"It's my Spanish-Mexican bloodline," he proudly explained. "I can go twenty-four, forty-eight hours and still keep this shine."

A quick, squeamish glance at Avery and he moaned: "Yeah. You look like shit."

Respect filled his eyes.

"But you did it."

The second floor was only half full at night, with most of the officers either at home or working the streets. The conference room lights were on. Dylan Connelly paced around inside, obviously upset. At the sight of them, he threw open the door.

"Where the hell have you been?!" he snapped. "I wanted a report on my desk at five o'clock. It's almost seven. You turned off your walkie-talkies. *Both* of you," he pointed out. "I might expect that from you, Black, but not you, Ramirez. No one called me. No one answered their phones. The captain is pissed too, so don't go crying to him. Do you have any idea what's been happening around here? What the hell were you thinking?"

Ramirez raised his palms.

"We called," he said, "I left you a message."

"You called twenty minutes ago," Dylan snapped. "I've been calling every half hour since *four thirty*. Did someone die? Were you chasing down the killer? Did God Almighty come down from Heaven to help you out on this case? Because those are the only acceptable answers for your blatant insubordination. I should take both of you off this case right now."

He pointed to the conference room.

"Get in there."

Angry threats were lost on Avery. Dylan's fury was background noise that she could easily filter out. She'd learned the skill long ago, back in Ohio, when she had to listen to her father scream and yell at her mother almost nightly. Back then, she'd held her ears tight and sang songs and dreamed about the day she would finally be free. Now, there were more important matters to hold her attention.

The afternoon paper lay on the table.

A picture of Avery Black was on the cover, looking startled that someone had just shoved a camera in her face. The headline read "Murder in Lederman Park: Serial Killer's Defense Attorney on the Case!" Beside the full-page image was a smaller picture of Howard Randall, the old and withered serial killer from Avery's nightmares with Coke-bottle glasses and a smiling face. The heading over his photo said: "Trust No One: Attorney Or Police."

"Have you seen this?" Connelly growled.

He picked up the paper and slapped it back down.

"*You're on the front page!* First day on Homicide and you're front page news—*again*. Do you realize how unprofessional this is? No, no," he said at Ramirez's expression, "don't even try to speak right now. You both screwed up. I don't know who you talked to this morning, but you stirred up a shitstorm. How did Harvard get wind of Cindy Jenkins' death? There's a memorial for her on Kappa Kappa Gamma's website."

"Lucky guess?" Avery said.

"*Fuck you, Black! You're off the case. You hear me!?*"

Captain O'Malley eased into the room.

"Wait," Ramirez complained. "You can't do that. You don't know what we've got."

"I don't care what you've got," Dylan roared. "I'm not finished yet. It just gets better and better. The Mayor called an hour ago. Apparently, he used to play golf with Jenkins' father, and he wanted to know why a has-been defense attorney—who got a serial killer released from prison—is dealing with the murder of a close friend's daughter."

"Calm down," O'Malley said.

Dylan spun around, red-faced and mouth open. At the sight of his captain—who was smaller and quiet but seemed coiled and ready to explode—he eased back.

"For whatever reason," O'Malley said in an even voice, "this case just blew up. Therefore, I'd like to know what you've been doing all day, if that's OK with you, Dylan?"

Connelly muttered something under his breath and turned away.

The captain nodded to Avery.

"Explain yourself."

"I never told anyone the victim's name," Avery said, "but, I did interview a girl from Kappa Kappa, Cindy Jenkins' best friend, Rachel Strauss. She must have put two and two together. I'm sorry about that," she said with a genuinely apologetic look to Dylan. "Small talk isn't my strong suit. I was looking for answers, and I got them."

"Tell them," Ramirez urged.

Avery moved around the conference table.

"We've got a serial killer on our hands."

"*Oh come on!*" Dylan lamented. "How can she possibly know that? She's been on the case for a day. We have *one* dead girl. There's no way."

"*Will you shut up?*" O'Malley yelled.

Dylan bit down on his lower lip.

"This is no ordinary murder," Avery said. "You told me as much yourself, Captain, and you must have seen it too," she said to Dylan. "The victim was made to look alive. Our killer worshipped her. No bruises on her body, no forced entry, so we can rule out gangs or domestic violence. Forensics confirmed that she was drugged with a powerful, probably a natural anesthetic the killer might have created himself, flower extracts that would have instantly paralyzed, and slowly killed. Assuming he keeps these plants underground, he'd needs lights, a water system, and food. I made some calls to find out how these seeds are imported, where they're sold, and how to get my hands on the equipment. He also wanted the victim alive, at least for a little while. I wasn't sure why, until we caught him on surveillance."

"What?" O'Malley whispered.

"We got him," Ramirez said. "Don't get too excited. The images are grainy and hard to see, but the entire abduction can be seen from two separate cameras. Jenkins left the party a little after two thirty on Sunday morning to go to her boyfriend's house. He lives about five blocks from the Kappa Kappa Gamma suite. Avery took the same walk she assumed Jenkins took. She noticed an alley. Who knows what possessed her to do it, but on a hunch, she checked a surveillance camera at a nearby smoke shop."

"You need a warrant for that," Dylan cut in.

31

"Only if someone asks for it," Avery replied. "And sometimes a friendly smile and engaging conversation go a long way. That shop has been vandalized about ten times in the last year," she went on. "They recently had an outside camera installed. Now, the store is on the opposite side as the alley, and it's about half a block down, but you can clearly see a girl—and I believed it was Cindy Jenkins—get accosted under some trees."

"That's when she called me," Ramirez took over. "Now, I thought she was crazy. Seriously. I saw the video and I wouldn't have blinked twice. Black, on the other hand, had me call forensics and bring in the whole team over this shit. As you can imagine, I was pissed. But," he said with excited eyes, "she was right. There's another camera at a loading dock in the back of the alley. We asked the company to let us see what was on it. They agreed and boom," he said and opened his arms wide. "A man comes out of the alley holding our victim. Same dress. Same shoes. He's slight of frame, shorter than Cindy, and dancing. He was actually holding her and dancing. She was clearly drugged. Feet dangling and everything. At one point, he even looks in the camera. That sick fuck was taunting us. He puts her in the front seat of a minivan and just drove away like it was nothing. The car is a Chrysler, dark blue."

"License plate?" Dylan asked.

"It's a fake. I already ran it. Must have had a dummy plate on. I'm compiling a list of all the Chrysler minivans in that color sold in the last five years within a five-county radius. It will take a while, but maybe we can narrow down the list with more information. Also, he had to be wearing a disguise. You could barely see his face. Wore a moustache, possible wig, glasses. All we can gauge is the height—around five-five or five-six—and maybe skin color: white."

"Where are the tapes?" O'Malley asked.

"Downstairs with Sarah," Avery responded. "She said it might take a while but she'll try to get sketch of the killer based on what she sees by tomorrow. Once we have facial recognition, we can compare it to our suspects and put it through the database to see what comes up."

"Where are Jones and Thompson?" Dylan asked.

"Hopefully, still working," Avery said. "Thompson is in charge of surveillance at the park. Jones is trying to track that car from the alley."

"By the time we left," Ramirez added, "Jones had found at least six different cameras within a ten-block radius from the alley that might be able to help."

"Even if lose the car," Avery said, "we can at least narrow down the direction. We know he turned north out of the alley. That, matched with whatever Thompson finds at the park, and we can triangulate an area and go house by house if we have to."

"What about forensics?" O'Malley asked.

"Nothing in the alley," Avery said.

"Is that it?"

"We've got some suspects, too. Cindy was at a party on the night of her abduction. A guy named George Fine was there. He's apparently been following Cindy around for years: takes classes she takes, seems to randomly bump into her at events. Kissed Cindy for the first time, danced with her all night."

"Have you spoken to him?"

"Not yet," she said and looked right at Dylan. "I wanted your approval before a potential shakedown at Harvard University."

"It's a good thing you have *some* sense of protocol," Dylan grumbled.

"There's also the boyfriend," she added to O'Malley. "Winston Graves. Cindy was supposed to go to his house that night. Never showed up."

"So we've got two potential suspects, footage of the event, and a car to track down. I'm impressed. What about motive? Have you given that any thought?"

Avery looked away.

The footage she'd seen, as well as the victim's placement and handling, all pointed to a man that loved his work. He'd done it before, and he'd do it again. Some kind of power trip must have motivated him, because he had little care for the police. The alleyway bow to the camera told her as much. That took courage, or stupidity, and nothing about the body dump or the abduction pointed to a lack in judgment.

"He's toying with us," she said. "He likes what he does, and he wants to do it again. I'd say he's got some kind of plan. This isn't over yet."

Dylan snorted and shook his head.

"Ridiculous," he hissed.

"All right," O'Malley said. "Avery, you're clear to talk to your suspects tomorrow. Dylan, contact Harvard and give them the head's-up. I'll call the chief tonight and let him know what we've got. I can also see about getting you some blanket warrants for cameras. Let's keep Thompson and Jones on their toes. Dan, I know you've been working all day. One more gig and you can call it a night. Get the addresses of those two Harvard boys if you don't have them already. Roll by on your way home. Make sure they're tucked in tight. I don't want anyone bolting."

"I can do that," Ramirez said.

"*OK*." O'Malley clapped. "Get going. Great job to both of you. You should be proud of yourselves. Avery and Dylan, hang out for a minute."

Ramirez pointed at Avery.

"Want me to pick you up in the morning? Eight? We'll head over together?"

"Sure."

"I'll keep on Sarah about that sketch. Maybe she'll have something."

The sudden eagerness of a partner to help—on his own and without prodding—was new for Avery. Everyone else she'd been paired up with since the moment she'd joined the force had wanted to leave her dead in a ditch somewhere.

"Sounds good," she said.

Once Ramirez had gone, O'Malley made Dylan sit on one side of the conference table and he had Avery sit on the other.

"Listen up you two," he said in a quiet yet firm voice. "The chief called me today and said he wanted to know what I was thinking, handing this case over to a well-known and disgraced former criminal defense attorney. Avery, I told him you were the right cop for the job and I stand by my decision. Your work today proves I was right. However, it's almost seven thirty and I'm still here. I've got a wife and three kids waiting for me at home and I desperately want to go and see them and forget about this miserable place for a while. Obviously, neither one of you shares my concerns, so maybe you don't understand what I'm saying."

She stared back at him, wondering.

"*Get along and stop bothering me with your bullshit!*" he snapped.

A tense silence blanketed the room.

"Dylan, start acting like a supervisor! Don't call me with every whiny detail. Learn how to handle your people on your own. And you," he said to Avery, "you better cut out the wacky humor act and the I-don't-give-a-shit attitude and start acting like you care for once, because I *know* you do." He stared at her for a long time.

34

"Dylan and I have been waiting on you for hours. You want to turn off your radio? Not answer phones? Maybe it helps you think? Good for you. You go right ahead. But when a superior calls, you call them back. The next time this happens, you're off the case. Understood?"

Avery nodded, feeling humbled.

"Understood," she said.

"Got it." Dylan nodded.

"Good," O'Malley said.

He stood taller and smiled.

"Now, I should have done this sooner but there's no better time than the present. Avery Black, I'd like you to meet Dylan Connelly, divorced father of two. Wife left him two years ago because he never came home and he drank too much. Now they live in Maine and he never gets to see his kids, so he's pissed off all the time."

Dylan stiffened and was about to speak, but said nothing.

"And Dylan? Meet Avery Black, former criminal defense attorney that screwed up and released one of the world's worst serial killer onto the streets of Boston, a man that killed again and destroyed her life. She leaves behind a multimillion-dollar gig, an ex-husband, and a kid that barely talks to her. And, like you, she's usually drowning her sorrows in work and alcohol. You see? You two have more in common than you think."

He turned deadly serious.

"Don't embarrass me again, or you're *both* off the case."

CHAPTER EIGHT

Left alone in the conference room together, Avery and Dylan sat across from each other for a few moments in absolute silence. Neither one of them moved. His head was low. A grimace lined his face and he seemed to be mulling something over. For the first time, Avery felt some sympathy for him.

"I know what it's like—" she began.

Dylan stood up so fast and stiffly that his chair slid back and hit the wall.

"Don't think this changes *anything*," he said. "You and I are nothing alike."

Although his menacing body language emanated anger and distance, his eyes said something different. Avery was sure he was on the verge of a breakdown. Something the captain had said affected him, just like it had affected her. They were both damaged, lonely. Alone.

"Look," she offered, "I just thought."

Dylan turned away and opened the door. His profile on the way out confirmed her fears: there were tears in his bloodshot eyes.

"Dammit," she whispered.

Nights were the worst for Avery. She had no steady group of friends anymore, no real hobbies other than the job, and she was so tired that she couldn't imagine doing more legwork. By herself at the large, blond table, she hung her head low and dreaded what came next.

The way out of the office was like every other day, only there was a charged feeling in the air, and many on the force were even more emboldened by her front page story.

"Hey, Black," someone called and pointed to her cover photo. "Nice face."

Another officer tapped on the image of Howard Randall.

"This story says you two were very close, Black. You into gerontophilia? You know what that means? It means you like to fuck old people."

"You guys are hilarious." She smiled and shot her fingers out like guns.

"*Fuck you*, Black."

* * *

36

A white BMW was parked in the garage; five years old, dirty and worn. Avery had bought it at the height of her success as a defense attorney.

What were you thinking? she mused. Why would anyone buy a *white* car?

Success, she remembered. The white BMW had been bright and flashy, and she wanted everyone to know she was a *boss*. Now, it was a reminder of her failed life.

Avery's apartment was on Bolton Street in South Boston. She owned a small two-bedroom on the second floor of a two-story building. The place was a downgrade from her former penthouse high-rise, but it was spacious and neat, with a nice terrace where she could sit and relax after a hard day's work.

The living room was an open space with shaggy brown carpeting. The kitchen was to the right of the front door, and separated from the rest of the room by two large islands. There were no plants or animals. A northern exposure ensured the apartment was usually dark. Avery threw her keys on the table and shed the rest of her belongings: gun, shoulder harness, walkie-talkie, badge, belt, phone, and wallet. She undressed on the way to the shower.

After a long soak to process the events of the day, she put on a robe, grabbed a beer from the fridge, then her phone, and headed out to the terrace.

Nearly twenty missed calls flashed on her cell, along with ten new messages. Most of them were from Connelly and O'Malley. There was a lot of screaming.

Sometimes Avery was so single-minded and driven she refused to pick up for anyone that wasn't essential to her task, especially when all of the pieces hadn't been put together; today was one of those days.

She scrolled down through last numbers dialed—and all the people that had called her in the past month. Not a single one was her daughter, or her ex-husband.

Suddenly, she missed them both.

Numbers were dialed.

The phone rang.

A message answered: "Hi, this is Rose. I'm not here right now to take your call, but if you leave a brief message, and your name and number, I'll get back to you as soon as I can. Thanks so much." *Beep.*

Avery hung up.

37

She toyed with the idea of calling Jack, her ex. He was a good man, her college sweetheart with a heart of gold: a truly decent person. They'd had a torrid affair when she was eighteen, and she, with a sickening ego after her dream job, had ruined everything.

For years, she blamed other people about the split, and for the rift with her daughter: Howard Randall for his lies, her old boss, the money, the power, and all those people she had to constantly entertain and beguile to stay one step ahead of the truth: Little by little, her clients had become less reliable, and still she wanted to keep going, to ignore the truth, to bend justice one way or the other—simply to win. Only one more case, she often told herself. Next time, I'll defend someone *truly* innocent and set the record straight.

Howard Randall had been that case.

I'm innocent, he'd cried at their first meeting. *These students are my life. Why would I hurt one of them?*

Avery had believed him, and for the first time in a long time, she had begun to believe in *herself*. Randall was a world-renowned psychology professor at Harvard, in his sixties, with no motive and no known history of his unhinged personal beliefs. More than that, he appeared weak and broken, and Avery had always wanted to defend the weak.

When she got him off, it was the highlight of her career, the highest of heights—that is, until he purposely killed again to expose her as a fraud.

All Avery had wanted to know was: why?

Why would you it? she'd asked him once in his cell. Why would you lie and set me up, just to go to prison for the rest of your life?

Because I knew you could be saved, Howard had replied.

Saved, Avery thought.

Is this salvation? she wondered and viewed her surroundings. Here? Now? No friends? No family? A beer in hand and a new life hunting down killers to make amends for my past? She took a swig of her drink and shook her head. No, this isn't salvation. At least not yet.

Her thoughts turned to the killer.

A picture of him had begun to form in her mind: quiet, lonely, desperate for attention, a specialist with herbs and corpses. She ruled out an alcoholic or drug addict. He was too careful. The minivan harked to a family, but his actions seemed to indicate a family was what he *wanted*, not what he *had*.

38

Her mind swirling with thoughts and images, Avery downed two more beers before she suddenly fell asleep in her cozy outdoor chair.

CHAPTER NINE

In her dreams, Avery was with her family again.

Her ex was an athletic man with cropped brown hair and dazzling green eyes. Avid climbers, they were on a hike together with their daughter, Rose; she was only sixteen and had already received an early admission to Brandeis College, even though she was only a junior in high school, but in the dream she was six. They were all singing and walking along a path surrounded by dense trees. Dark birds fluttered and cried out before the trees morphed into a shadowy monster and a knife-like hand stabbed Rose in the chest.

"No!" Avery screamed.

Another hand stabbed Jack and both he and her daughter were hoisted away.

"No! No! No!" Avery cried.

The monster lowered.

Dark lips whispered in her ear.

There is no justice.

Avery jolted awake to the sound of incessant ringing. She was still on the terrace in her robe. The sun had already come up. Her phone continued to blare.

She picked up.

"Black."

"Yo Black!" Ramirez answered. "Don't you ever pick up? I'm downstairs. Get your shit together and get out here. I've got coffee and sketch samples."

"What time is it?"

"Eight-thirty."

"Give me five minutes," she said and hung up.

The dream continued to permeate her thoughts. Sluggishly, Avery rose and headed into the apartment. Her head pounded. Faded blue jeans were tugged on. A white T-shirt was made respectable by a black blazer. Three chugs of orange juice and a downed granola bar was breakfast. On the way out, Avery glanced at herself in the mirror. Her attire, and her morning meal, were a far cry from thousand-dollar suits and daily breakfast at the finest restaurants. Get over it, she thought. You're not here to look pretty. You're here to bring in the bad guys.

Ramirez handed her a cup of coffee in the car.

"Looking good, Black," he joked.

As always, he appeared to be the model of perfection: dark blue jeans, a light-blue button-down shirt, and a dark-blue jacket with light-brown belt and shoes.

"You should be a model," Avery grumbled, "not a cop."

A smile displayed his perfect teeth.

"Actually, I *did* do a little modeling once."

He pulled out of the breezeway and headed north.

"You get any sleep last night?" he asked.

"Not much. How about you?"

"'I slept like a baby," he said proudly. "I *always* sleep well. None of this gets to me, you know? I like to let it *ride*," he said and waved his hand through the air.

"Any updates?"

"Both boys were home last night. Connelly put a watch on them just to make sure they didn't bolt. He also talked to the dean to get some information and make sure no one freaks out about a bunch of plainclothes cops hanging around campus. Neither kid has a file. Dean said they're both good boys from good families. We'll see today. Nothing yet from Sarah on the facial recognition. We should hear something this afternoon. A few dealerships called me back with names and numbers. I'm just going to keep a list for a while and see what happens. You see the morning paper?"

"No."

He pulled it out and threw it on her lap. In big, bold letters, the headline read "Murder at Harvard." There was another picture from Lederman Park, along with a smaller photo of the Harvard campus. The article inside rehashed the editorial from the previous day and included a smaller picture of Avery and Howard Randall from their days in court together. Cindy Jenkins was mentioned by name but there was no photo given.

"Slow day in the news?" Avery said.

"She's a white girl from Harvard," Ramirez replied, "of course it's big news. We gotta keep those white kids safe."

Avery raised a brow.

"That sounds vaguely racist."

Ramirez vigorously nodded.

"Yeah," he agreed, "I'm probably a little racist."

They wove through the streets of South Boston and headed over the Longfellow Bridge and into Cambridge.

"Why'd you become a cop?" she asked.

"I *love* being a cop," he said. "Father was a cop, grandfather was a cop, and now I'm a cop. Went to college and got bumped up

41

quick. What's not to love? I get to carry a gun and wear a badge. I just bought myself a boat. I go out on the bay, chill out, catch some fish, and then catch some killers. Doing God's work."

"Are you religious?"

"Nah," he said, "just superstitious. If there *is* a god, I want him to know I'm on his side, you know what I mean?"

No, Avery thought, I don't.

Her father had been an abusive man, and while her mother faithfully went to church and prayed to God, she was more of a fanatic than anything else.

The voice from her dream returned.

There is no justice.

You're wrong, Avery replied. And I'm going to prove it.

* * *

Most Harvard seniors lived off-campus in some of the residential housing units owned by the school. George Fine was no exception.

Peabody Terrace was a large high-rise set along the Charles River near Akron Street. The white, twenty-four-story building included an expansive outdoor patio, beautiful lawns, and a clear view across the river for those students lucky enough to be placed on the higher floors; George was one of them.

A number of buildings connected Peabody Terrace. George Fine lived in Building E on the tenth floor. Ramirez parked his car along Akron Street and they made their way inside.

"Here's his picture," Ramirez said. "He should be asleep right now. His first class isn't until ten thirty."

The image was a smaller crop of a larger picture pulled of the Internet. It showed a disgruntled, extremely cocky student with oily black hair and dark eyes. A slight grin was on his face; he seemed to be challenging the photographer to find a flaw with his perfection. A strong jaw and pleasant features made Avery wonder why he was called a weirdo. He looks confident, she thought. So why stalk a girl that obviously has no interest in him?

Ramirez flashed his badge at the doorman.

"You got problems?" the doorman asked.

"We'll know soon enough," Ramirez replied.

They were waved up.

On the tenth floor, they turned left and walked down a long hallway. Carpets were tan brown swirls. Doors were painted glossy white.

Ramirez knocked on Apartment 10E.

"George," he said, "you around?"

After a brief silence, someone said: "Get lost."

"*Police*," Avery interrupted and banged on the door. "Open up."

Silence again, then ruffling and then more silence.

"Come on," Avery called. "We don't have all day. We just want to ask you a few questions."

"You got a warrant?"

Ramirez raised his brows.

"Kid knows his stuff. Must be *ivy* educated."

"We can have a warrant in about an hour," Avery called out, "but if you make me leave and jump through hoops, I'm going to be pissed. I already feel like shit, today. You *don't* want to see me pissed off, too. We just want to talk about Cindy Jenkins. We heard you knew her. Open the door and I'll be your best friend."

The bolt unlocked.

"You really *do* have a way with people," Ramirez realized.

George appeared in a tank top and sweatpants, extremely muscular and toned. He was about 5'6", the same height Avery associated with the killer based on Cindy's records. Despite the look of someone that was either on drugs or who hadn't slept in days, a fearlessness burned in his stare. Avery wondered if he'd been bullied for years and had finally decided to strike back.

"What do you want?" he said.

"Can we come in?" she asked.

"No, we can do this right here."

Ramirez put his foot inside the room.

"Actually," he said, "we'd rather come in."

George looked from Avery to Ramirez—to the foot holding the door open. Resolved, he shrugged and backed away.

"Come on in," he said. "I have nothing to hide."

The room was large for a double occupancy, with a living space, terrace, two beds on opposite sides of the room, and a kitchen area. One bed was neatly made and piled with clothing and electronic equipment; the other one was a mess.

George sat on the messy bed. Hands beside him, he gripped the mattress. He appeared ready to lurch forward at any moment.

Ramirez stood by the terrace window and admired the view.

"This is some place," he said. "Only a studio, but grand. Look at this view. *Wow*. You must love looking out at the river."

"Let's get this over with," George said.

Avery pulled a chair and sat down facing George.

"We're looking into the murder of Cindy Jenkins," she said. "We thought you might be able to help us, seeing as you were one of the last people to see her alive."

"A lot of people saw her alive."

The words were meant to sound tough, but there was pain in his eyes.

"We were under the impression you liked her."

"I *loved* her," he said. "What does that matter? She's gone now. No one can help me."

Ramirez and Avery shared a look.

"What does that mean?" Ramirez asked.

"The way I understand it," Avery said, "you left the party right after her."

"I didn't kill her," he declared, "if that's what you mean. I left the party because she practically stumbled out of the door. I was worried about her. I couldn't find her when I got downstairs. I had to say goodbye to a few people. Ask around. That's the truth."

"Why would you need to say goodbye to anyone?" Ramirez asked. "If you were in love with her, and worried, why wouldn't you just help?"

"Talk to my lawyer."

"You're hiding something," Ramirez pointed out.

"I didn't kill her."

"Prove it."

George lowered his gaze and shook his head.

"She ruined my life," he said. "She ruined my life and now you're trying to ruin my life too. You think you're so important."

Ramirez gave Avery a look as if to say *this kid is loco!* and moved out to admire the spectacular view from the terrace.

Avery knew better. She'd seen his type before, both as an attorney and a cop. There was something damaged about him, and powerful. Coiled and ready to strike, she thought, just like some of the gang members she'd interviewed: an innocence mixed with indignation that quickly turned to violence. A hand went to her belt. Her fingers slid close to her holster without actually making a move toward the gun.

"What did you mean by that, George?" she asked.

44

When he looked up, his body was flexed. A wild grimace marred his features. Eyes were wide and lips pulled in. He cringed. On the verge of tears, he sucked it back.

"*I matter,*" he cried.

A cocky swagger took over. He stood up and extended his arms wide. Tears came and surprised him, and he then he gave in to the tears.

"*I matter,*" he sobbed and squatted down.

Avery stood up and moved away, hand close to her gun.

"What's this all about?" Ramirez asked.

"Leave him alone," Avery said.

Oblivious to the desperation that reeked out of their broken suspect, Ramirez squatted down beside George and said: "Hey, man, it's OK. If you did it, just admit it. Maybe you're crazy or something. We can get you help. That's why we're here."

George stiffened and went still.

A whisper came from his lips.

"I'm not crazy," he said, "I'm just sick of you people."

As deftly as a trained soldier, a hand went behind his back and pulled a hidden blade. In the next instant, he spun around Ramirez and clinched his neck. He quickly stabbed his right side, just below his chest, and as Ramirez screamed out, George sank back into a sitting position, using Ramirez as a shield.

Avery drew her weapon.

"*Don't move!*" she called.

George held the blade to Ramirez's temple.

"Who's the loser now?" he said. "*Who!?*" he screamed.

"*Drop it!*"

Ramirez groaned from the wound between his ribs. The arm around his neck clearly made it difficult for him to breathe. He reached for his gun but the point of the blade pressed deeper into his temple. George hugged him tight and whispered in his ear.

"Be still."

A groan from Ramirez and then he screamed out.

"*Shoot this fucker!*"

Avery watched as George pressed the knife tight against Ramirez's head, and a trickle of blood began to flow—and in that moment, she knew she had no choice. It was her partner's life or this creep's—and any second could make the difference.

She fired.

Suddenly, George screamed out in pain and went stumbling backwards, releasing his grip on Ramirez.

Avery looked over and saw him covered in blood, grabbing his shoulder. She was relieved to see it was a clean shoulder shot, just as she had hoped.

Ramirez scrambled to get his gun, but before he could react, suddenly George was back up on his feet. Avery couldn't believe it. Nothing could stop this kid.

Surprising her even more was that George did not charge Ramirez, or her.

He was charging for the open balcony.

"WAIT!" Avery screamed.

But there was no time. He had a good ten feet on her, and she could see from his sprint that he was going to jump.

Again, she made a hard choice.

Again, she fired.

This time, she aimed for his leg.

He went down, face first, grabbing his knee, and this time he didn't get back up. He lay there, groaning, feet from the balcony.

Ramirez stood and whirled around. With a hand on his wound, he grabbed his gun and pointed the muzzle at George's face.

"You fuckin' cut me!"

"I've got him," Avery said.

Ramirez threw a kick to George's side and Ramirez cringed from the pain as he did so, holding his wound tighter.

"Fuck!" he screamed.

On his side on the ground, George smiled, blood pouring from his lips.

"Did that feel good, *cop*? I hope it did, because I'm going to get out of this."

Avery stepped forward, pulled out her cuffs, yanked his arms behind his back, and clamped them tight.

"You," she said, "are going to jail."

46

CHAPTER TEN

Avery called 911 with her gun trained on George. She used her walkie-talkie to dial backup. Ramirez couldn't get over how stupid he'd been, or how much the wound actually hurt. Every so often, he'd shake his head and mumble to himself.

"Can't believe this punk got the jump on me."

"He's fast," Avery said. "You have training, George? Army? Navy? Is that how you were able to abduct Cindy?"

George sat cross-legged and silent with his head low.

"How's the wound?" Avery asked Ramirez.

"I don't know. I can breathe, so maybe he missed the lung. But the fucker hurts."

He then stopped and looked at her with awe.

"Thanks, Black. You had my back. I owe you one."

When the ambulance arrived, the EMT applied pressure to the wound and asked Ramirez a few questions. The initial diagnosis was that the knife might have missed the lung. The entire time, Ramirez kept shaking his head. "Stupid," he said. "Stupid."

A gurney was brought in to take him away.

"I'll be back," he said to Avery. "Don't worry. This is nothing. Just a scratch. Hey, George," he called out. "You assaulted a cop. That's six years maximum. And if you killed a little girl, you get life."

Harvard security stayed with Avery until the police came for George. Nobody spoke the entire time. Avery had been around killers before, lots of killers, in her three years on the force, but it was kids with guns and knives that always gave her pause: kids like George. College student. Harvard University. Someone that seemingly had it all, and yet on the inside he was fractured, broken.

Once the cops came and took George away, Avery stood alone in the apartment. The word "why" kept going through her head.

Why did he do this?

Why? Why? Why?

The face of Howard Randall kept appearing. What's wrong with this world? she wondered. Look at this place. Sky view. Luxury all the way. Young, good-looking, physically fit, and yet he just attacked and stabbed a police officer. Other faces came to mind: gang faces and angry husbands and drunken psychos that killed innocent people and other kids, some six years old with Uzis strapped around their chests.

47

Why?

Was it pain? The pain of such a hard life?

A memory came: her father, unkempt gray hair, missing teeth, a shotgun in his hand. "You want to talk about *pain*?" he'd snapped. "I'll shoot you in the fucking head! Then you'll know pain, won't you, girl? *Won't you!?*"

Avery stood up.

It had been had been hard to focus on the apartment until everyone was gone. Now she made the room, and George Fine, her top priority.

Who are you? she asked.

The walls were practically bare except for one picture of George, proudly displaying a medal he'd won for a race. On his desk, Avery found keys and a wallet. At least ten keys were on the chain. What do you need all these for? she wondered.

No password locked his computer. A check of his recent Internet activity proved useless: a bunch of porn videos, relationship advice, and workout locations around campus. Two social networking sites were open. He had thirty-two friends on one of them. Mr. Popularity, she sarcastically thought.

Hidden in his closet was a box full of pictures: George with a group of men in the woods all wearing Army Reserve T-shirts; George between his parents with Harvard in the background; and Cindy Jenkins, hundreds of photos of Cindy Jenkins: Cindy at the mall, Cindy in Harvard Yard, Cindy at a party. Every photo appeared to have been taken in secret, from afar, or sometimes from right beside her, without her knowledge.

"Jesus."

Anger welled up inside of her, not at the find or what George might have done if left unchecked, but at Harvard, the dean, and a life of secrecy that had nearly killed her partner.

A few minutes searching on her phone and Avery dialed a number.

"I want to speak to Dean Isley, right now," she said.

"I'm sorry," the assistant replied, "the dean is in a meeting."

"*I don't care if he's on the fucking moon,*" Avery snapped. "This is Avery Black, Boston PD, Homicide. I'm standing in the room of one of your students: George Fine. Does Isley know about George? He must, because your 'normal' Harvard senior just stabbed a cop. Get him on the phone right now!"

"Hold, please."

Two minutes later, the dean came on.

48

"Hello, Detective Black," he said, "sorry about the wait. I've just been briefed on your activities this morning."

"I just want to understand something," Avery said. "My supervisor, Dylan Connelly, called you last night for a background check on George Fine and Winston Graves. You said, and I quote my partner here, the one that was stabbed, 'They're both good boys from good families.' Do you want to revise that statement?"

The dean cleared his throat.

"I'm not sure what you're asking," he said.

"Really? Because I think I'm being crystal clear. Let me say it in another way. We've got one downed cop. We've got one dead girl. Now we have a prime suspect who *you said* wasn't a problem. I'm giving you one last opportunity to revise your statement before I seriously consider pressing charges. I just discovered George Fine was an army reserve. That might have been relevant information, don't you think? He's also a trained martial artist. Again, relevant. Good boy from good family just doesn't cut it. What else do you know about him?"

"Officer Black, our relationship to our students is—"

"Tell me now or I hang up and you're on your own."

"Ms. Black, I can't just—"

"Five…four…at one I hang up…"

"We have—"

"You have a dead girl and a possible murderer on your hands…three…two…"

"All right!" he yelled, flustered.

His voice went low.

"Now mind you," he said, "no one here actually believes that one of our students could possibly be responsible for—"

"He stabbed a cop. My partner. Tell me what you know."

"He was on disciplinary probation his first two years at the college," the dean admitted. "He'd followed a young girl here from Scarsdale: Tammy Smith. There were…problems. No charges were filed. We didn't want the press. He was under strict orders to stay two hundred yards away from her and have weekly meetings with our school psychologist. I was under the impression his sessions were going well. He's been a model student ever since."

"Anything else?"

"That's all. The files are here if you care to look through them."

'What about Winston Graves?"

"Graves?" The dean nearly laughed, "He's one of our top seniors, a standout in every way. I hold him and his family in the highest regard."

"No secrets?" Avery pushed.

"Not that I'm aware."

"That means maybe," Avery said. "I'll check on my own. And the next time a cop calls you for information, you might want to be as forthcoming as possible. 'Cop stabbed in Harvard dorm' probably isn't a great headline for school admissions."

"Wait a minute, I thought we—"

Avery hung up.

The next call was to Jones, a skinny, humorous Jamaican who complained about everything, even when he was having the time of his life.

"Jones here," he said.

"This is Black. Where are you on the street surveillance?"

Jones was cramped in a dark office space surrounded by two technicians in blue. He leaned forward on his keypad and cocked his eyes like he was about to jump off a roof.

"You crazy, Black," he complained. "You know that, right? How much longer I gotta do this maddening shit? It's like a guessing game out here. I have to *guess* where he might have gone, then I gotta access those cameras and punch in the right times and see what happens. Hours and hours I stare at nothing. Only once I get lucky."

"You got lucky?"

"Yeah," he said and watched the screen. "I'm in traffic control right now with Stan and his girlfriend Frank. These guys are great. They helping me out all day. So here's what I do. I accessed the cameras on the street lights on Auburn, at Hawthorn. You know what I find? I find your minivan. He go straight up Auburn, past Hawthorn. I check on Auburn further west, just past Aberdeen, and I see the minivan again. He's heading west."

"Where did he go after that?"

"Are you fuckin' serious!" Jones cried. "What I look like? I ain't no satellite imagery system over here! That took me like, five hours!"

"Keep on it," Avery said and hung up.

The minivan was headed west, she thought. Out of the city. If George is our guy, he definitely had a house somewhere.

Her next call was to Thompson, longtime partner of Jones, a huge, brutish man who looked almost albino from his coloring, with

50

blond hair, full lips, and the facial features of a woman. Thompson was kicked back in an office with a bunch of state troopers, eating donuts and telling a story about when he caught Jones sleeping and painted a bunny face on him.

"Thompson," he answered in a deep voice.

"It's Black. What's the update?"

"The minivan headed north up Charles Street. That's all I've got. Wasn't sure if I should check the bridges or not."

"We've got a murderer on the loose," Avery snapped. "You check *everything*. Your partner Jones is already way ahead of you. Where did he go after Charles Street?"

"Let me figure that out," he said.

"No," she replied. "You're off surveillance duty for the day. I need you on something more important: George Fine. Harvard student. I'm here now. Ramirez's been stabbed. He's at the hospital. I need everything you can find on George Fine. Contact his parents if you have to. He's in police custody. Does he have a house somewhere, maybe northwest of Harvard? Keys are right here on his desk. Any previous medical history? Talk to his friends, family, anyone you can, you understand? No password on his computer so you can go through that too. You're on Harvard duty for the rest of the day."

"I'll be there in a minute."

"No—you'll get here *now!*" she yelled and hung up.

North, she thought. He went north from Lederman Park. Maybe over the bridge and right into Harvard? Then why would you go west after you picked up Cindy from the alley?

Talk to me, Fine, she thought and gazed around the room. Talk to me.

* * *

An hour later, Avery was at the hospital.

The knife had only slightly perforated Ramirez's lung. Luckily, it had missed all the other major organs, but doctors needed to go in and stitch up the internal wound.

She headed to the waiting room.

Three plainclothes cops were already there. One of the cops had a frog-like face; he was pudgy but solid, with cropped black hair and narrow eyes.

Great, Avery thought. Finley.

Finley Stalls was one of the worst bullies in the department, a deeply unhappy Irishman who drank every night and walked around the office in a foul mood every day. He had a sardonic sense of humor, and although he was never the first person to pick on Avery, he was always the last one laughing.

All three officers gave her the same emotionless expressions that she was used to in the department. She was about to wave and try to dilute their typical charm when Finley nodded in her direction and spoke in his fast, practically incomprehensible Boston accent.

"Wicked good work," he said.

She couldn't tell if he was kidding or not.

The second officer chimed in.

"You trying to get the record for most partners killed, Black?"

Ah, she thought. Kidding.

"Come on," the third officer scoffed. "Give her a break. It's not her fault. Ramirez is a fuckin' fairy around suspects. Always acts like the hand of God won't get him hurt or something. Fuckin' idiot. She got him here in one piece, didn't she?"

"You catch the killer?" the second officer asked.

"We'll see," Avery said.

She waited for the next joke, the next verbal assault, but none came. The officers simply mulled around, and for the first time in a long time, Avery was able to mentally relax around a bunch of cops and try to focus.

She called forensics.

"Randy, any updates?"

Randy sat in a white lab in the basement of the department. A microscope was on her desk and she peeked through it while she talked.

"I'm glad you called," she said. "Remember those natural drugs we talked about, the plants he might have had to paralyze and ultimately kill his victim? I received confirmation on that. The toxins in her body pointed to about sixty percent opium. Very pure. Has to be his own plant. Did you get any leads on that?"

"I talked to a drug supplier I know," Avery said. "Asked who would be stupid enough to sell just the poppy seeds and have their heroin sales go down the drain. Waiting to hear back. I was hoping you had some other leads. I'm nowhere on LED lights and gardening supplies. You can get them anywhere."

"Looking at fibers right now taken off the girl's body," Randy said. "One of them is definitely cat, maybe a tabby? I think our killer likes animals. Hopefully, he doesn't just stuff them for show.

There are dirt specks, too. Typical garden variety. I'd say you're looking for a green thumb, and someone that has plants, animals, a real garden nut."

Avery couldn't fit the pieces together.

George Fine had no plants and no cats.

Maybe it's at his other location, she thought. But wouldn't there have been *some* evidence of that in his dorm? Books on botanicals, drugs?

"All right," Avery said. "Call me if you find anything else."

* * *

Later in the afternoon, Avery knocked on Ramirez's door and entered.

Ramirez waved her in with his arms high and a smile.

"Look who it is," he called. "My savior."

"Not really," Avery replied. "What did I do?"

"You kept your cool," Ramirez pointed out, "and you acted like a real cop with a suspect in there, not some stupid rookie like me. It's all good, though," he scowled, "I'll be out of here in no time. Doctor said I can leave tomorrow. I'll be back at the desk by Friday."

"That's not what I hear," Avery said. "Doctor said you need at least two weeks to heal. He wants you off your feet."

"What?" Ramirez complained. "You better not tell the captain about that. Don't make me go home and sit on my ass. You don't know what my home life is like."

"What's your home life like?" she wondered.

Ramirez was an enigma to her: good-looking, in great shape, perfectly dressed, and seemingly bothered by nothing. The attack by George had shown another side: a bit careless, angry, and no real defensive training to have dealt with George's speed and surprise. At first, he'd reminded Avery of all the men she'd had random one-night stands with a few years back. They, too, had been shiny on the outside, but once she'd peeled back a layer or two, they were a mess. She hoped that wouldn't be the case with her new partner.

"Aw, man, you really want me to dispel the mystery?" he said. "OK, why not. I *am* in a hospital bed. I know I come off like Superman, but honestly? I'm just a normal guy on the inside, Black. I love the job but I don't like to sweat, so I'm rarely in the gym and I'm definitely not the most deadly man on the force. You see this amazing physique? I was born with it."

53

"Anybody at home?" Avery asked.

"Used to have a girlfriend. Six years. She left me a while back. Said I had too much trouble committing. Come on, Black! Let's be honest. Why would a man as fine as myself commit to one woman, when there are millions out there?"

Lots of reasons, Avery thought.

She remembered Jack, her ex-husband. Although they hadn't spoken in a long time, the urge to marry him had been strong when she was younger. He'd offered stability, kindness, love, and support. No matter how intense or aloof Avery had become, he was always there, waiting and eager to give her a hug.

"I guess people commit because they want to feel safe," she said.

"That's no reason to commit," he said. "Gotta be for love."

Avery had never really understood the concept of love until her daughter Rose was born. As a young college student, she thought she'd loved Jack. The feelings were there and she missed him when he wasn't around, but if she'd really been in love, she wouldn't have taken him for granted so much, or left.

She had Rose when she was barely twenty. Jack had wanted to start a family early, but when Rose was born, Avery had felt trapped—no more time alone with Jack, no more time for herself, no more life, career. It had been a mess. *She'd* been a mess, and it had showed—the end of her marriage, the end of her being a mother. But even though she and Rose were still estranged, she knew, now, she knew.

"What do you know about love?" she asked.

"I know it means I have to make my woman feel good." He smiled with a sheepish, seductive stare.

"That's not love," Avery said. "Love is when you're willing to give up something you care about for someone else. It's when you care more about the other person than your own desires, and you act on it—that's love. It has nothing to do with sex."

Ramirez raised his brows in respect.

"Whoa," he said. "That's deep, Black."

The memories were painful for Avery to recall. Instead, she tried to stay focused on the task at hand: a killer on the loose and a suspect in custody.

"I gotta go," she said. "Just wanted to make sure you were going to be all right. All I need is another dead partner on my hands."

"Go, go," Ramirez said. "Where's our Navy Seal?"

54

"In custody. And you're actually not that far off. He's army reserve. Very good with his hands. I already lambasted the dean for withholding information about a possible lethal weapon. Thompson is over at the dorm now."

"You think he's our killer?"

"I'm not sure."

"What's the hesitation?"

Pieces, she thought. Puzzle pieces that didn't fit.

"He could be our guy," she said. "Let's see what happens."

CHAPTER ELEVEN

An hour later, Avery stood in a small, dark side chamber with O'Malley and Connelly. Ahead of them, through one-way glass, sat George Fine. His hands were handcuffed to a metal table and he had bandages on his shoulders and legs from the gunshot wounds. He was lucky, Avery realized, that she had just grazed him. Her aim had been true.

Every so often he muttered something under his breath, or twitched. Blank eyes sought out nothing but seemed deep in thought.

In her hand, Avery held a picture that displayed six different black-and-white interpretations of a man's face, based off the surveillance videos of the killer. Each picture showed a Caucasian perpetrator with a narrow chin, high cheekbones, small eyes, and a high forehead. In three of the photos, the wig, glasses, and moustache had been removed, and the artist had given the killer various hairstyles and facial hair. The last three images maintained at least one aspect of the disguise in case it *wasn't* a disguise.

Avery took time to absorb every photo.

The face she'd seen on the cameras was embedded in her mind, and now, with a bunch of clear sketches, she was able to infer other looks: a wider chin, lower cheekbones, a bald head, larger eyes, glasses, and multiple colors for the eyes.

Every so often, she looked up Fine. There were similarities: Caucasian, high cheeks… He seemed to have a leaner frame, but they were both light on their feet. The graceful movements Avery had seen on camera were a lot like the ones she'd observed when George overtook Dan. Still, Avery wasn't sure. There were the plants and animals. Also, the killer on camera had a fiendishness about him, a spritely humor that was lacking in George. Would George Fine have bowed to a camera?

As if Connelly could mentally hear her doubts, he pointed at the window and said: "This is our guy. I'm sure of it. Look at him. He's barely said two words since he came here. Can you believe he wants a lawyer? *No way.* He gets nothing. We need a confession."

O'Malley had on a dark suit and red tie. He pulled at his lips and frowned and said: "I might have to agree with Connelly on this one. You said you found pictures of Jenkins in his room. He attacked and nearly killed a cop. He also fits the profile. Those sketches are a near match. What's the hesitation?"

56

"The pieces don't all add up," she said. "Where did he take Cindy after the abduction? How did he learn how to embalm? Randy Johnson said those hairs on Jenkins' dress were from a cat. Fine doesn't own a cat. What he does have is a lot of Internet searches for porn and relationship advice. Does that sound like a killer?"

"Listen, Black, this is a courtesy here," Connelly said with finality. "As far as I'm concerned, this case is over. We got him. He must have a safe house somewhere. That's where we'll find the cat and the minivan and the murder weapon. Your job is to find that house. Jeez, why do you always have to act like you're so much better than everyone else?"

"I just want to get it right."

"Yeah? Well, that wasn't always the case, was it?"

A feral energy pulsed from Connelly, cheeks red, eyes bloodshot as if he'd been drinking or had a rough night. He was busting out of his shirt, as usual, and he appeared ready to punch someone in the face.

She addressed O'Malley.

"Let me talk to him."

"He's your perp." O'Malley shrugged. "You can do what you want. But we think this is our guy. We've got a lot of people breathing down our necks on this one. Unless you can prove something else, and quick, let's wrap this up, OK?"

She gave him the thumb's-up.

"You got it, boss."

The door to the interrogation room buzzed and Avery pushed through. Everything was gray, including the steel table where the shooter sat, and the mirror and walls.

George blew out a frustrated breath and lowered his head. He wore the same tank top and sweats.

"You remember me?" Avery asked.

"Yeah," he said, "you're the bitch that pointed a gun in my face."

"You tried to kill my partner."

"Self-defense." He shrugged. "You busted into my room. Everybody knows Boston PD have itchy trigger-fingers. I was just trying to protect myself."

"You stabbed him."

"Talk to my lawyer."

Avery took a seat.

"Let me see if I can get this straight," she said. "You're an economics major. Average student. Army reserve. No criminal record, well, at least not before today. By all accounts, a quiet, harmless student. Only a few friends." She shrugged. "But I guess that's what you get when you're not a hard partier in college. Successful parents. One lawyer. One doctor. No siblings, *but*," she noted with emphasis, "a history of hard crushes. Yeah," she almost apologized, "I talked to the dean and learned all about your crush on Tammy Smith, the girl you followed from Scarsdale? Is she the reason you went to Harvard, or was that just coincidence?"

"I didn't kill anyone," he said, and looked her right in the eyes with a determined, unrelenting gaze as if he dared her to say otherwise.

Nothing about the interview felt right to Avery.

Instinct told her she'd already made the correct assessment: he was unstable and lonely, a teenager on the verge of a breakdown before the girl of his dreams was suddenly murdered, and then he snapped. But a meticulous murderer that drained bodies and put them in angelic, lifelike positions? She had trouble believing it. There was just no solid proof.

"Do you like movies?" she asked.

He frowned, uncertain about her line of questioning.

"Can you tell me what's currently playing at the Omni Theatre?" she added. "The cinema across from Lederman Park?"

A blank expression greeted her.

"There are three movies playing there," she answered. "Two of them are 3D summer action flicks. I don't really care about those," she said with a flick of her wrist. "The third is called *L'Amour Mes Amis*, a little French film about three women who fall in love with each other. Have you ever seen that movie?"

"Never heard of it."

"Do you like foreign films?"

"Talk to my lawyer."

"All right, all right," she said. "How about this? One more question. You give me an honest answer and I'll leave here and get you a lawyer. OK?"

He said nothing.

"No strings attached," she added. "I'm serious."

Avery took a moment to formulate her thoughts.

"You could be my killer," she said. "You really could. We have a lot of avenues to still explore but some of the pieces add up. Why

58

else would you attack a cop? Why is your room so clean? Makes me think you have another place somewhere. Do you?"

An unreadable stare greeted her.

"Here's my problem," Avery said. "You could also just be a stupid kid that was destroyed over the death of a crush. Maybe you were furious and miserable, and obviously a little unstable because you attacked a cop. But," she emphasized and pointed to the two-way glass, "my supervising officer and my captain both think you're guilty of first-degree murder. They want to see you burn. I'm going to give you a choice. Answer one question for me and I'll rethink my position and give you what you want. OK?"

She leaned forward and peered deep into his eyes.

"Why did you attack my partner?"

A complex set of emotions passed through George Fine. He frowned and mulled over his words, and then he looked away and back at Avery.

A part of him seemed to be calculating a response, and figuring out what that response would mean in a court of law. Finally, he settled on something. He moved in closer, and although he tried to act tough, his eyes were glassy.

"You all think you're so big, so important. Well, I'm important too," he said. "My feelings matter. You can't just say we're friends and then ignore me. That's confusing. I'm important too. And when you kiss me, that means you're mine. *Do you understand?*"

His face cocked and tears rolled down his cheeks and he screamed:

"That's means you're mine!"

59

CHAPTER TWELVE

He checked his watch. It was close to six o'clock.

The sun was still out and people were everywhere on the massive lawn.

He sat against a tree along Killian Court on the MIT campus. Easily seen among the shade of the high foliage, he wore a cap and glasses.

His destination had been reached only a few minutes before. Problems at the office had facilitated a last-minute spreadsheet for his boss. Often, he asked the All Spirit why his boss couldn't be killed, as well as anyone else he deemed a nuisance. Without a word—only through strange sounds and disturbing images—the All Spirit had let him know that *his* thoughts and feelings were meaningless: all that mattered were the girls.

Young. Vibrant. Full of life.

Girls that could release the All Spirit from his prison.

A temple of girls, college girls ready to take on the world, a spring well of thriving, potential energy easily given over to the All Spirit, enough power to break through his interdimensional realm and reach the Earth as a physical presence. No more need for apostles and minions. Freedom. At last. And all those who helped him? Those who were patient and strong, who had built the temple of these young college morsels out of love and care? What about them? Well, they would be assured a place in Heaven, of course, as gods in their own right.

It was Tuesday, and on Tuesday night, Tabitha Mitchell always went to the great dome library to study with friends after class.

At six fifteen, he spotted her. Tabitha was half Chinese and half Caucasian. Pretty and popular, she was laughing with friends. She flipped her dark hair and shook her head at something that was said. The group walked across the lawn.

There was no need to follow. Her destination was already known—back to the dorms to change, and then out to the Muddy Charles Pub for the Tuesday Special: Ladies Night. All girls drink for free. Tuesday was her favorite night to party.

He took a sip of a smoothie, closed his eyes, and mentally prepared.

* * *

60

The build-up was his favorite part, the waiting, the yearning, and the near explosion of his desire. Love was an emotion easy to feel with these girls. Every one of them had vivacity of spirit and energy and an incredible purpose they all shared, bigger than anything they could have ever achieved on their own. They were princesses in his mind, queens, worthy of his adoration and perpetual worship.

The rebirth was hard for him.

After they'd been changed, they were no longer his own. They had moved on to become sacrifices for the All Spirit, building-blocks in the temple of his eventual return, so all he had to remember them by were pictures, and the memories he had of a budding love cut too short, as always cut too short.

He stood along the Charles River and stared out at the rolling waves of water. Night had come and he was always the most introspective at night, before the induction. Behind him, across Memorial Drive, Tabitha Mitchell walked with her friends to the Muddy Charles Pub. They would stay there for at least two hours, he knew, before they all split apart and Tabitha headed back to her dorm, alone.

Stars were barely visible in the dark sky. He spotted one, then two, and he wondered if the All Spirit lived in those stars, or if he was the sky itself, the universe. As if in answer, he saw the image of the All Spirit: a darker shadow among the sky that seemed to encompass the entire sky. There was a patient, expectant look on the All Spirit's face. No words were spoken. All was understood in that moment.

At around nine, the killer headed back toward the pub and waited on a narrow passage between the bar, which was in the large, white-columned building of Morss Hall, and the Fairchild Building. The area wasn't well lit. A number of people ambled about.

At nine thirty-five, she appeared.

Tabitha said her good-byes in front of the hall. At the bottom of the steps, they all went their separate ways. Her two friends turned toward their apartment on Amherst Street, and she turned right. As was her habit, she moved into the passway.

Regardless of the many people nearby and on the street, the spirit of an actor embodied the killer. He took the persona of a drunkard and ambled over to Tabitha. In the palm of his hand, attached to his fingers by silver rings, he cupped a handmade plunger-needle.

Quickly passing behind her, he simultaneously stung the back of her neck, gripped her neck so she wouldn't move, and pulled her in close.

"Hey, Tabitha!" he said in a very familiar, loud, phony British accent, and then, to lower her guard, he added, "Shelly and Bob told me you'd be here. Let's make up? OK? I don't want to fight anymore. We belong together. Let's sit down and talk."

Initially, Tabitha jerked and attempted to dislodge herself from the assailant, but the quick-acting drugs made her throat numb. In the seconds that followed, the names of her friends confused her. Combined with the dwindling speed of her mind and body, she hopefully thought that her sorority sisters were playing some kind of joke.

He was meticulous about how he held her. One hand wrapped around her back to catch her from a fall. The other hand, which held the anesthetic, placed the needle into his right cargo pants pocket, and then he cupped her cheek. In this way he held her up with his strong arms and continued to talk as if they were truly an arguing couple on the verge of a possible mend.

"Are you drunk again?" he declared. "Why are you always drinking when I'm gone? Come here. Let's sit down and talk."

At first, many people on the street or walking through the grassy breezeway—directly past the killer and Tabitha—believed something was obviously wrong: her unnatural movements said as much. A few even stopped to watch, but the killer was such an expert in his handling of Tabitha's body that after the initial injection and her brief struggle, Tabitha appeared like any other intoxicated college student being helped by a best friend or lover. Her feet tried to walk. Her arms grasped at him—not in an aggressive way but as if she were in a dream and needed to shoo clouds.

Gently, lovingly, the killer led her over to a wall, sat down with her, and stroked her hair. Even the most watchful and vigilant passersby soon assumed everything was fine and continued on with their evening.

"We'll be happy together," the killer whispered.

He kissed her softly on the cheek. The excitement he felt was even stronger than with Cindy. Strangely aroused, he peered up into the dark sky to see the All Spirit, watching him with a grimaced look of disapproval.

"All *right*." The killer blanched.

A deep hug brought Tabitha closer to his body. He smelled her scent, squeezed her arms and legs. Slight moans came from her lips, but he knew they would be fleeting; the drugs would erase her mind in just over twenty minutes.

Two boys played Frisbee Golf right beside them. A group of rowdy college freshmen sang songs. Cars raced by along the Charles River.

Amid the populated area, the killer picked Tabitha up and slung her over his shoulders for a piggy-back ride. Although her feet dangled, he held her hands on his chest and jogged to his car, which was parked on Memorial Drive.

"Come on!" he cried in his accent. "Put your legs around me! You're making me do all the work. At least help me out a little bit? *Please?*"

He continued the dialogue by the blue minivan, where he rested her on the car, opened the passenger door, and gently placed her inside.

For a few seconds, he remained squatted by the door, not only to keep up the concerned-boyfriend charade, but to observe her features, to watch her chest rise and fall, and to wonder—as he had so often—what it would be like to kiss her, for real, and to make love. The All Spirit grumbled from his heavenly position, and the killer, with a sigh, closed the passenger side door, took his place by the steering wheel, and drove away.

CHAPTER THIRTEEN

On Wednesday morning, bright and early, Avery entered the office to check her messages and see if any new leads had come in. The disturbing interview with George had only confirmed one thing: he was crazy. Could he be the killer? Sure, Avery had begun to suspect, but there were still other avenues she needed to pursue.

One last suspect remained: Cindy Jenkins' boyfriend, Winston Graves. Graves was a Harvard fencing champion from an elite family. His father owned a number of supermarket chains and his mother was a regular on QVC. By all accounts, he was a dedicated student and athlete who would never have to work a day in his life, but he still received top grades and had aspirations of representing his country in the Olympics.

Slim, she thought, but worth checking out.

"Hey, Black," the captain called, "come on in here."

Finley Stalls sat before the captain's desk, like a thief about to be caught red-handed. Despite their brief moment of camaraderie the day before, Avery wanted nothing to do with him. A beat cop usually assigned to whatever homicide squad division was in need, he was, she believed, lazy, mean, untrustworthy, and he had an accent so thick and fast it was nearly impossible to understand what he was saying half the time.

"What's up, Cap?"

O'Malley wore a navy blue long sleeve shirt and tan slacks. Stubble lined his face and he appeared to have gotten little sleep.

"Looks like Thompson kicked down the right doors," he said. "We received a call this morning from Shelly Fine, mother of our assumed perp. Looks like she lent him some money to rent out a cabin on Quincy Bay for the entire month. Here's the address," he said and handed her a slip of paper. "That might be our spot. Get down there now. If this is it, I'll meet with the chief this afternoon to schedule the news conference."

Avery checked the address.

Southwest, she thought, on the water. Far from the abduction site or car routes. Intel from Jones had the killer driving in the opposite direction after the alleyway in Cambridge. And Thompson had the car going north.

"Sure," she said, "I'll head there this afternoon."

64

"What are you? Drunk?" he snapped back. "I just handed you the potential address of our killer, and you tell me you'll wait until this afternoon?"

"Thompson and Jones spent most of the day yesterday going over car routes. They had the minivan heading north from the park and west from the alley. Not once did it veer south. I'm not saying Fine isn't our killer. I just think."

"Listen, Black. You can *think* all you want. You want to follow-up on other leads? You go right ahead. *After* you search this cabin. You hear me? As far as I'm concerned, this case is over. I want it tied up with a pretty ribbon on top. You better make me look good for the chief."

"Sure," she said, "no problem."

"That 'sure' sounds a lot like 'I'll do what I want,'" O'Malley said. "Look, *Avery*," he said and settled down, "I know you're smart. That's why you were promoted, yeah? And I know you've got great instincts. But what I need now is closure. If I'm wrong? Great. Rub it in my face all you want. But for now? We've got the best lead so far and I expect you to follow it."

"Understood," she said.

"Good," he replied, "now take your new partner and get out of here."

"Finley?"

"Yeah," he said. "You got a problem with that?"

"Seriously?"

"What?" the captain challenged. "You think I'm giving you a *good* cop? Your first partner was killed. Your second one is in the hospital. Finley is perfect. Solves all my problems. If he does good? Great. If he gets killed? Not a problem. I can at least tell the chief I finally got rid of some dead weight around here."

"I'm right here!" Finley yelled.

O'Malley pointed at him.

"Don't you disappoint me," he snapped. "I'm tired of it, you hear me, Fin? You prove yourself on this case and maybe I'll rethink my opinion about your dedication as an officer. For now, you're just a racist cop that gets moved around from department to department because no one wants to fire you. Is that what you want? You like that title? *Good.* No more jerking around. You do what she says and clean up your act. Understand?"

* * *

65

"What crawled up his ass?" Finley snapped when they'd left. The words were spoken extremely fast, and with such a heavy accent that Avery thought it sounded like "Whacawlup-is-ass" and she had to take a minute to figure it out.

She was at least a head taller than Finley and seemed like a supermodel compared to him with his frog-like lips, chubby cheeks, large eyes, and short, stout frame.

Barely a word was spoken until the reached the car.

The white BMW seemed to offend Finley.

"Whoa!" he shouted. "I'm not getting in that thing."

"Why not?"

"It's a girly car."

Avery hopped inside.

"Suit yourself."

Finley—completely out of his element in his blue patrol uniform standing next to a white convertible BMW—appeared as dejected as a kitten in a rainstorm.

"Hey, Fin," a distant cop shouted. "Nice ride."

"Ah, man," Finley moaned.

"It's called karma," Avery said when Finley begrudgingly hopped in and closed the door. "What comes around goes around."

She headed out of the lot and turned west.

"Hey," he said, "where you going? Quincy Bay is in the other direction."

"We'll get there," she said.

"Now wait a minute," Finley complained. "I was in that office too. Cap said we go to Quincy Bay. No exceptions."

"He also said you need to listen to me."

"No way. No way," Finley shouted. "You can't screw this up for me, Black. Turn the car around. This is my last shot. Captain hates me. We gotta do what he says."

His dropped consonants and verbal speed made Avery shake.

"Do you ever listen to yourself?" she asked. "I mean, do you ever record yourself and then go back and try to understand what you said?"

Finley looked lost.

"Forget it," she motioned.

"Black, I'm serious," he pushed.

"Have you ever encountered a serial killer?" she asked.

"No. Yes. Well, maybe." Finley thought.

"There's something about them," Avery said, "something different from other people. I didn't know that until I represented

66

one as a lawyer and thought he was innocent. After it turned out that I was wrong, I started to see things differently. His house, what he collected. On the outside, they looked like normal things, but in hindsight, they were clues. A shadow veiled everything," she remembered, "a shadow that longed to be lifted."

"What the fuck are you talking about?" Finley whined.

Avery breathed out a heavy sigh.

"George Fine might be our killer," she said. "He stalked girls and he attacked a cop. But what I saw around him, it doesn't add up. Points to something different, like a crazy kid who's stuck in his own head. There's no solid proof of anything else, which makes me think the house is a getaway, some place he goes to try and get out of his own head. I don't know, maybe I'm wrong. We'll get to the house. I promise. Just give me an hour."

Finley shook his head.

"Shit, man, I'm fucked."

"Not yet," she said. "Just a brief detour to Harvard to interview one final suspect and then it's on to Quincy Bay."

Dead silence lasted the rest of the way into Cambridge. At one point, slightly curious about Finley and their difficult past together, Avery cocked a brow and asked a question.

"Why are you always such an asshole?"

"To you?"

"Yeah, to me."

Finley shrugged as if the answer was obvious.

"You're a chick," he said. "Everyone knows chicks don't make good cops. Heard you were a lesbian too. You like to bang serial killers, right? Crazy shit. You're a crazy chick, Black. Besides, you always look like you belong somewhere else. So I say to myself: why doesn't she go work somewhere else if she don't like it here? That's all. Busting your balls. Gotta fight back if you want respect," he said and punched the air. "Pop, pop, pop."

Avery began to wonder if he was slightly special.

* * *

"Can I help you with something?"

Winston Graves looked just like he'd been portrayed by the sorority girls: cocky, aloof, tall, dark, and athletic. He had dreamy green eyes and a toned, tan body. Although not a perfect match to the man Avery had seen in the surveillance videos, she tried to

67

imagine him in disguise and slumped over to make him seem shorter.

On the porch of his first-floor apartment house, he wore white and red basketball shorts, flip-flops, and a tank-top. Books were in his hand. He glanced over at Finley, who stood further away on the sidewalk and glared at Winston like a pit bull ready to strike.

'My name is Avery Black," she said and flashed her badge. "I'm with Homicide. I'd just like to ask you a few questions about Cindy Jenkins."

"It's about time," he said.

"What do you mean?"

"I called the cops on Sunday. This is the first time anyone thought it might be important enough to talk to me? *Huh*," he fake laughed, "I'm touched."

"I'm not sure I understand," Avery said. "Did you have anything to add to the case? Is that why you wanted the police to call you back?"

"No," he said, "I'm just forever amazed at the stupidity of our public servants."

Avery winced.

"Ouch," Finley said. "You better mind your smart-ass tongue, Harvard boy, or I'll bring in your clean ass for Obstruction."

Winston looked over at Finley, haughty at first; but then when he caught a good look at his raging eyes, he seemed to show the slightest bit of self-doubt and humility.

"What do you want?" Winston demanded.

"You can start by telling me where you were Saturday night," Avery said.

Winston laughed.

"Are you serious?" he said. "I'm a suspect now? This just gets better and better."

A powerful, protected air surrounded Winston, like he was untouchable, above them all, and blessed by money and birthright. He reminded Avery of all the multimillionaires she'd worked with as an attorney. During that time in her life, she probably acted just like him.

"Just going through the motions," she said.

"I was playing poker with my friends. Everyone was at my house until about midnight. You want to check? Go right ahead. Here are some names," and rattled off a few of his Harvard classmates.

Avery took notes.

"Thanks for that," she said. "And, how are *you*?"

He frowned.

"What's that supposed to mean?"

"I don't know, just trying to be empathetic. How are you feeling? I assume this must have been very difficult for you. The way I understand it, you and Cindy were in a long-term relationship. Two years, isn't that right?"

"Great detective work," he said sarcastically. "Cindy and I were over. Not officially, but in the past few months, it became painfully obvious that we were not meant to be together. We were moving in different directions. I was going to break up with her. So no, I wasn't that broken up. It's a terrible tragedy. I was upset when I heard what happened, but if you're looking for tears, you came to the wrong place."

"Wow," Avery said. "It's only been three days."

"I'm sorry," Winston snapped, "is there something I'm missing here? You come to *my* house, make me feel like I'm a suspect, question my relationship, and then try to make me feel guilty about my emotions? You might want to be careful with your words, Detective, or I'll call my lawyer and make sure you're put on a tighter leash."

"*Shut your fuckin' mouth!*" Finley yelled with a pointed finger.

Avery flashed him a look that said "you are *not* helping."

Her phone rang.

"Black," she said.

O'Malley was on the line.

"Stop whatever you're doing," he said in an urgent, soft-spoken tone. "Turn the car around and head over to Violet Path in the Mount Auburn Cemetery over in Watertown. Plug it into your phone and get there now. Ask for a detective named Ray Henley. He's in charge. The cabin can wait."

"What is it?" she asked.

There came a three-second pause.

"They just found another body."

CHAPTER FOURTEEN

Mount Auburn Cemetery was a luxurious property of winding roads, lakes, and lush forests with gravestones strewn throughout.

A number of Watertown police cruisers, along with unmarked cars, an ambulance, and a forensics van, made it impossible to drive very far into Violet Path. Trees obscured most of the overhead sunlight. Multiple groups of onlookers and bikers craned their necks to see something just outside of Avery's view. She parked at the bottom of a grassy knoll, just at the intersection of Walnut Avenue and Violet.

"Hey you," a plainclothes cop shouted when she exited her car, "you can't park there. Move that car. This is a crime scene."

Avery flashed her badge.

"Avery Black," she said, "Homicide. Boston PD."

"You're out of your jurisdiction, Boston. We don't need you here. Go home."

Avery smiled: reasonable and pleasant.

"I was told to contact Ray Henley?"

"Lieutenant Henley?" Suspicious, the officer grumbled, "Wait here."

"What's up his ass?" Finley interjected.

He stood right behind Avery, practically against her shoulder.

"Am I being punished?" she asked. "Is that why you're here?"

"This is my big break, Black. You're going to help me reach detective."

"God have mercy on my soul."

A lean, attractive man in slacks and a red plaid shirt came over the hill. He looked more like an outdoorsman than a detective; only the badge around his neck and the gun on his hip gave it away. He had a sunburned face and wavy brown hair. An aura of wellness and patience exuded from his being, and he smiled at Avery as if they knew each other.

"Detective Black." He waved. "Thanks for coming."

A strong hand gripped hers, and when he peered into her eyes, a calm feeling came over Avery, like she could sink into his arms and instantly be forgiven for all her sins.

An awkward pause followed.

"I'm Ray Henley?" he said.

70

"Right," Avery replied, flustered, "sorry. I was told you found another body, similar to the one we discovered over in Lederman Park?"

Her immediate discussion of the case turned him off slightly, and he breathed a wistful sigh and rubbed his cheeks.

"Yeah," he said, "come up and see for yourself."

He updated her on the way.

"A runner found her this morning around six. For a second, she thought the girl was some kind of Satan worshiper from the way she was positioned. We believe her name is Tabitha Mitchell, an MIT junior that never showed up at her dorm last night. Her roommate called the police around two, and then again eight. Cambridge police would have normally waited forty-eight hours to post a picture but since she's a connected college student, we caught a break."

"What's she doing out here?"

"I thought *you* could help us with that."

The body was at the top of the knoll. Small gray tombstones marked the area. She was draped over a larger stone that resembled a chess piece pawn. He had once again done incredibly lifelike work. She was squatted and hugging the monument. Her cheek rested on the top. Eyes were open and there was a lasciviousness about her appearance. Red blush painted her cheeks. Some kind of glue had been sprayed on her forehead and hair tips to imitate sweat, and her mouth was puckered in a sense of breathlessness.

"She's not wearing any undergarments," Ray said.

Cindy Jenkins wore undergarments: panties and a bra. What does that mean? Avery wondered. Is the killer becoming bolder? Did she just leave the house that way?

Tabitha's eyes were open and focused on something in the distance.

Avery tracked the line of sight to a bunch of white, short tombstones on an opposite, grassy decline.

"Finley," she said, and inwardly bristled at his name, "write down whatever you see on those graves over there. Mark them down so I know which one's first, second, third, got it? Then take a walk around the area. Serial killers usually return to the scene of the crime to get a cheap thrill. Maybe ours is still here."

"A serial killer?" He beamed. "Oh wow. You got it, Black," and he flashed her a can-do attitude and pointed a finger in her face to express seriousness.

"Is that your partner?" Ray asked.

71

"No," she insisted.

Once again, he tried to start a conversation.

"Saw you in the paper a couple of days ago." He smiled. "*And*," he emphasized, slightly embarrassed, "I saw you in a *lot* of papers a few years ago."

His implication wasn't clear until Avery glanced at him and realized: He's flirting.

It was hard for her to do anything in front of a dead body except analyze what happened and try to piece together the puzzle. She wondered if that was some kind of mechanical flaw born from her past guilt and torment, but then she remembered she'd always been that way, even as an attorney: focused, relentless, and eager to find the connections that would lead to success. Now, the only difference was that those connections weren't just ways to get her clients off—they were ways to stop murderers.

Ray sensed her discomfort and changed the subject.

"You think this is your guy?"

Avery cleared her throat.

"Absolutely," she said. "This is his work."

"Well then," he sighed, "I'll share whatever we have. We don't get many crime scenes like this in Watertown. And, if you like, we can even have the body sent to your lab and you can take things over from there. You OK with that?"

"Of course," she said, genuinely appreciative. "That would be great."

"Don't get the wrong idea," he added with a smile, "I'm not just a nice guy. Truth be told? I'm a little OCD when it comes to sharing. It makes my skin crawl trying to imagine two sets of paperwork on something this important, and timely."

"Still," she offered, "thank you."

He held her look for as long as possible; Avery blushed and turned away, excited by the attention but eager to get back to work. Thankfully, another officer flagged him down.

"Lieutenant, we have a situation over here."

"Be right back," Ray said.

The cemetery was peaceful, calming, just like the area where Cindy Jenkins was placed in Lederman Park. Why? Avery wondered. What's the significance of parks? Mentally, she checked off avenues to pursue: Was Tabitha a sorority girl like Cindy? She's a junior, and half Asian. So the killer can't be hunting down seniors, or specifically white girls. Cindy came from an established family. What about Tabitha? They were both abducted from Cambridge.

72

Why? Is that where the killer lives? Where was Tabitha last seen? Who saw her alive? Can we get surveillance? The list seemed endless.

What do we *know*? she pushed.

Nothing, she mentally replied. We know absolutely nothing.

No, she rallied, we know *something*: the relative size and shape of the killer, his ethnicity, MO, and the specific drugs he used. Ramirez was compiling a list of hallucinogenic plant suppliers, as well as car dealerships and Internet sites that sold Chrysler blue minivans. We can pursue those leads. We can also share the killer's sketch with Cambridge police. See if there's a match. We can also try to track that minivan from Lederman.

I just need more people, she thought. And *not* Finley.

Police sirens blared.

Cops spun into action.

"We got a runner! We got a runner!"

Farther off, on another path visible from her position, a black car, maybe a Mustang, revved up and burned smoke out of the cemetery. Ray was below shouting orders. Two police officers and a photographer around the body perked up and started to head toward the action.

"*No, no,*" Avery called and pointed. "You stay here. Someone has to guard the body."

Finley, she thought. Where is Finley?

Her walkie-talkie buzzed to life.

"Hey, Black," came Finley's voice, "we got him! I got him!"

"Where are you?" she demanded.

"I'm in a Watertown police cruiser with—hey, what's your name," he said to someone. "Shut up, man!" came a different voice. "I'm trying to drive!" "I don't know," Finley added, "some cop. We're the first ones out. Following a black Mustang. Heading northwest out of the cemetery. Hop in that pretty white pony of yours and back us up. We got him!"

CHAPTER FIFTEEN

Avery jumped in her car and stuck a siren on the roof. The red light whirled. Her walkie-talkie, a new model as sleek and small as a cell phone, was thrown aside. Instead, she turned on the car transreceiver and clicked the frequency she'd been assigned to Finley.

The car started. A backup curve and she hit the pedal and peeled forward out onto Walnut Avenue. The paths in the cemetery were a maze-like jumble. Through distant trees, she caught the tail end of a police cruiser. She abandoned the road and jumped onto the grass. Shit, she thought, I'm going to get into trouble for this. Headstones were avoided. The car turned onto another paved road and she was behind a pack of police vehicles.

Avery followed the chase out of the cemetery and onto Mt. Auburn Street. She narrowly avoided two cars. A crash resounded behind her. The line of red and blue police lights shifted onto Belmont Street.

Avery picked up her transreceiver mouthpiece.

"Finley," she called, "where are you?"

"Oh man," Finley replied, "you guys are way behind. We're ahead of everybody. This is great. We're going to catch this son of a bitch."

"*Where are you?*" she demanded.

"On Belmont, just past Oxford. No wait. He's turning onto Marlboro Street."

Avery checked her speedometer. Sixty-five…seventy. Belmont went in two directions. Her side was a one-lane street with enough room to slip by any slow cars on the right. Thankfully, all the police cruisers had already diverted traffic. She caught up to the last car.

"Made a left on Unity Avenue now," Finley called.

The line of police turned right on Marlboro and then made a quick left.

"We stopped. We stopped," Finley cried. "I'm out of the car. Mustang on the lawn of a small brown house, left side. Heading into the house."

"*Don't* go into the house!" Avery shouted. "Do you hear me? Do *not* go in!"

The line went silent.

"*Shit,*" she said aloud.

All the police cars had converged on a single brown two-story house with a short lawn and no trees. The Mustang had nearly smashed into the front staircase. The police cruiser beside it, Avery assumed, had been the one with Finley inside.

Avery hopped out and pulled the Glock out from her shoulder strap. Other officers had their weapons drawn. No one seemed to know what was happening.

"Is this our guy?" Henley called out.

"We don't know," another cop answered.

Yelling came inside.

Shots were fired.

"You two!" Henley roared to his men. "Go around back. Make sure no one leaves. Sullivan, Temple, keep your eyes on me."

He squat-ran up the stairs and into the house.

Avery made a move to go after him.

"*Hold up. Hold up*," a cop shouted.

Finley exited the house with his arms wide in pleasant victory, gun in hand.

"That's right," he said. "Game over for the serial killer."

"Finley, what happened?" Avery shouted.

"I got him," he declared, no sense of remorse or social etiquette. "Shot that mother-fucker. He pulled a weapon and I shot him. Saved some cop's life *and* shot his white ass. That's how we do it on the *south side*," he declared and threw up a gang symbol Avery immediately recognized as the South Boston D-Street Boys.

"Slow down," she said. "How do you know he's our guy?"

Finley cocked his neck and opened his eyes wide.

"Oh yeah," he declared, "That's our guy all right. Caught him in the basement. Lot of sick shit down there. You gotta see it to believe it."

Henley came out of the house.

"Sullivan," he called, "get an ambulance out here, now, and get down in that basement. Dickers was shot. He needs support. Travers," he said, "I want this place sealed off. No one in. No one out. You hear me? We don't need anyone else contaminating the scene. Marley! Spade" he yelled to the back. "Get out here."

"I need to see what's in there," Avery said.

"Go," Henley waved, "she's OK, Travers. Both of them," he indicated Finley. "No one else." And to Finley he added: "I'm going to need a statement from you, young man."

"No problem," Finley said. "Heroes tell tales."

"Tell me everything, slowly," Avery snapped.

Finley—still on an adrenaline rush—was hyped and bouncy.

"I did what you asked," he said in his speedy, accented tone, "wrote down those tombstone names. A bunch of girls, maybe eighteen or twenty years old. I don't know. I'm no good at math. Died in WWII. Then I saw this old guy watching everything from afar. Looked shady, you know? I alerted one of the other cops, because I'm a team player and all, and we went over to have a little chat. We get about halfway toward this guy and he bolts: hard run to the car. Who knew old people could run so fast? Jumps in and peels out. Wait until you see what we found. Solved the case single-handedly," he said and slapped his chest. "Don't worry. I'll give you some props," he added. *"Who's lazy now?!"* he yelled to the sky.

All Avery heard was "tombstones...girls...died in WWII..." and she made a mental note to find out everything about those markers and the women they served.

Gun drawn, Avery moved through the front door.

The house had an old, musty scent to it, like someone hadn't lived there in a long time. Carpets were dusty white. A staircase led to the second floor. Through the ceiling, Avery heard footsteps and someone yell, "Clear."

"Down this way," Finley said.

He led her around the stairs. A kitchen was on the left. To the right was a door that led to the basement. The scent was strong around the door: rotting corpses and scented oils. Oils, Avery thought; maybe this *is* our guy.

Creaky steps led to an expansive, dark basement with a stone floor. The smell was so strong Avery nearly retched: dead bodies and decomposition mixed with sweet-smelling fragrances to hide the scent. Air fresheners hung everywhere between the beams and exposed padding of the ceiling. Boxes lined nearly every wall, hundreds and hundreds of boxes. The only empty space held a long table marred with dried blood and cutting implements

Towards the back was a soiled bed.

A dead body lay on the bed, practically blue and decomposed from time, legs splayed open and tied to posts, along with the hands. It was a girl, someone young that Avery guessed had died years earlier.

Strange, sexual devices surrounded the area: bondage chairs; chains from the ceiling, and a swing. One of the boxes in the back was opened. Avery peeked inside and caught a glimpse of a woman's body parts.

76

She held her nose from the stench.

"Jesus."

"What did I tell you?" Finley beamed. "Crazy shit, right?"

A man lay dead at the foot of the wooden-post bed, 6'2" or 6'3". He was old and lean, with long gray hair. Maybe sixty, Avery thought. A shotgun was by his hand.

The downed cop sat against a side wall being aided by his friend. Luckily, he'd worn a vest, but some of the shotgun shells had gone through his neck and face.

"My wife's going to fucking kill me," the cop said.

"Nah," the other cop replied, "you're a hero."

The basement was dirty. Dust balls were everywhere. The tools on the desk, the desk itself, even the sex equipment had obviously never received a thorough cleaning. Boxes along the back were soiled and nearly falling over.

"I need to make a sweep," Avery said. "Finley. Check the garage. See if you can find our blue minivan, and disguises, plants, needles: anything related to our case."

"On it," he said and bounded up the stairs.

The rest of the house appeared old and unlived in, with no pets and no plants. It was neat, tidier than the basement, but still caked in dust. No indication of any other perversions could be found on the higher floors. Pictures that lined the walls were quaint copies of artists like Bruegel and Monet. The suspect, it seemed, spent most of his time on the second floor, where Avery found his personal effects and clothing.

She headed outside.

The neighborhood had come alive. Police lights still turned. Crowds had gathered around the areas sectioned-off area.

Finley came panting back.

"Just an empty garage with a lot of junk lying around," he said.

A picture of the killer had already taken shape in Avery's mind, based off what she'd seen on the surveillance tapes and what she believed from previous experience. She imagined a strong, dainty young man—educated and anti-social, a man that liked art and had a mind for medicinal concoctions. The way he placed his women were like Parish paintings, or works by Alphonse Mucha. Similarly, the drugs he administered were artlike in their own way, drawn from a number of rare, illegal plants and flowers. He was also fastidious about details, and clean, just like the placed bodies with their washed clothing and clean skin.

This house?

77

The man dead in the basement?

George Fine?

They were all pieces of the puzzle, but they felt like different puzzles, with their own pieces, and all the pieces were strewn together.

CHAPTER SIXTEEN

The police department stood on their feet when Avery and Finley appeared from the elevator banks. Finley basked in the attention. He bowed, hooted at his friends, and repeatedly yelled: "I'm the man, right? You see how we do it on the South Side?"

"Great job." People clapped.

"You got him!"

In a dark place, Avery heard none of it. The office was a shell with no one inside, the sounds: white noise. Images swirled in her mind: George Fine, Winston Graves, and the old dead man in his sick, twisted basement of horrors.

O'Malley came out of his office to personally shake Avery's hand.

"Talk to me," he said. "How did it go?"

"Guy's name is Larry Kapalnapick. Works at Home Depot as a loader," Avery said. "From the looks of it, all the bodies in the basement were already dead."

"Fuckin' grave digger!" Finley chimed in.

"He must have been doing it for years," Avery said. "Watertown police estimated there were body parts from at least twenty different people down there. Best guess is, he digs up a body, plays around for a while, and then cuts it up and stores it in the basement. Henley's department is having everything shipped to the lab just to make sure."

"Son of a bitch," O'Malley whispered.

Finley laughed.

"Motherfucker had Pine Scents hanging all over the basement ceiling."

"What about *our* victim?"

"We went back to the scene after the chase. Coroner was there and forensics. Randy says it was the same perpetrator as Cindy Jenkins, same MO, and from the smell of it, probably the same anesthetic. She'll check into that here."

"So, Fine isn't our guy."

"Can't be," she said. "He was locked up tight the night before. He's guilty of something. But not this. As a precaution, I asked Thompson and Jones to check out the cabin in Quincy Bay. Then Jones will continue street surveillance for the minivan, and Thompson has been assigned to dig up everything he can on Winston Graves."

79

"Graves? Jenkins' boyfriend."

"It's a long shot," Avery admitted. "In the meantime, Finley takes over on the Tabitha Mitchell case. He can start now with friends and family."

"Finley?"

"He worked his ass off today."

To Finley she added: "Remember to think *beyond* Tabitha Mitchell. We need any connections between her and Cindy Jenkins. Childhood history. College majors. Favorite foods. After-school activities. Friends and family. Anything."

With a fire in his eyes, Finley banged on his heart.

"I'm your pit bull," he said.

The captain nodded at her.

"What are *you* going to do?"

Avery imagined the blue minivan heading west from Boston. She believed the killer had to reside in one of the counties that followed: Cambridge, Watertown, or Belmont. The combined populations of those counties totaled almost two hundred thousand. An endless sea of faces.

"I need to think," she said.

* * *

Avery sited her Glock 27 at a distant target. Orange goggles covered her eyes. Plugs had been stuffed into her ears. She imagined the face of Howard Randall as a placeholder for the new, faceless killer. She fired.

Pop! Pop! Pop!

Three shots hit the target almost dead center.

Thinking had always been her strong suit: time away from a case when she could decompress and process what she knew.

A blank wall greeted her this time.

No leads. No connections. Just a wall that kept her away from the truth. Avery had never believed walls. Walls were for other people, other attorneys, other cops that simply didn't know how to break through those walls and see what others couldn't.

What am I missing?

Pop! Pop! Pop!

Her bullets faded to the right. At the start of her session, she'd hit nothing but bull's eyes. Now they were off. Just like you, she thought. *Off.* Missing the target. Missing something.

No, she mentally rallied.

Breathe in…breathe out…
Pop! Pop! Pop!
All bull's eyes.
Howard Randall, she thought.
Suddenly, she realized: That's it. A fresh perspective.
Stupid, she thought. *Crazy.* Connelly would go nuts. The media would have a field day. Fuck the media. Would he even do it? Of course he would; she knew for certain. He went to jail for you. He has this sick fascination about you. He's probably following the case already. No, she swore. I won't do it. I won't go down that road again.
She put in a fresh clip in her gun.
She fired.
Pop! Pop! Pop!
Every shot went wide.

* * *

In the darkness of the police station, well past midnight, Avery sat hunched over her desk. Pictures lay spread out before her: Cindy Jenkins, Tabitha Mitchell, Lederman Park, the cemetery, and the alleyway and screenshots of the minivan and the killer.
What am I missing?
Photos were meticulously analyzed.
Finley had already taken a few sworn statements. From the early looks of it, Tabitha had been abducted right out in the open, just like Cindy, probably only steps away from the bar she visited every Tuesday night. Only, there was no boyfriend or frequent stalker to question. According to those interviewed, Tabitha had been single for a while. Tabitha was in a sorority—Sigma Kappa—but the connections to Cindy Jenkins ended there. Tabitha was a junior economics major. Cindy was a senior in accounting.
Sororities.
Is *that* the link?
She made a mental note to check nationwide sorority gatherings.
The movie playing at the Omni was about three women. The gravestone pointed to three women. Does that mean he kills in threes? The movie and the WWII tombstone girls were compared and contrasted for any leads.
She surveyed multiple car routes around Cambridge and Watertown and imagined where the killer might live, and why he

81

might have chosen those routes. The list of dark blue Chryslers was now being supervised by Finley. They already had two thousand listed with owners for cars made and sold in the past five years. What if he bought it six years ago? she thought. Or seven?

Howard Randall continued to invade her thoughts. She even imagined she heard his voice: "You can come to me, Avery. I won't bite. Ask me your questions. Let me help you. I've *always* wanted to help."

She banged on her head.

"Go *away!*"

Still, the image came, and laughed.

CHAPTER SEVENTEEN

At seven-thirty the next morning, Avery sat in her car a half block down from the home of Constance and Donald Prince.

They lived in Somerville, just northeast of Cambridge, in a small yellow house with white trim on a quiet suburban street. A white picket fence surrounded the property. There were two porches: one on the first floor up, and another on the second level, where chairs and a table had been set for sunlit morning breakfasts.

The scene appeared to be the perfect setting: trees lined the sidewalks, the sun was coming up, and birds chirped in the sky.

Screams were all Avery could remember, the endless screams from the one and only time she had visited the Princes, and tears and plates being thrown against the wall as both of them had desperately tried to drive her away.

Constance and Donald Prince were the parents of Jenna Prince, the last Harvard student killed by Professor Howard Randall, nearly four years ago. The murder had come only weeks after superstar defense attorney Avery Black had done the impossible and gotten Professor Randall off for the murder of two other Harvard students, despite the overwhelming circumstantial evidence stacked against him.

Those brief few days between Avery's jury win and the killing of Jenna Prince resounded in Avery's mind. At the jury verdict, the celebration had begun. Nights were spent downing expensive bottles of wine and sharing her bed with numerous, nameless faces. One night in particular, she'd even called her ex to ask if he wanted to get back together again. She never even waited for a response. Avery had just laughed after her question and swore she'd never be with a loser like him again. The shame she felt over that moment continued to burn on her cheeks even now, years later.

Her victory had been short-lived.

She learned the truth from the papers a few days later: "Freed Harvard Killer Strikes Again." Like his previous victims, the many body parts of Jenna Prince had been carefully reconfigured near Harvard landmarks. But unlike the other murders, this time, Howard Randall had immediately stepped forward. He appeared in Harvard Yard almost as soon as the body was discovered, hands up in surrender and covered in blood. "This is for you, Avery Black," he had told reporters. "This is for your freedom."

And her belief that she was a decent, honorable person? That she'd finally done good and freed an innocent man?

Gone.

Everything she believed in was destroyed. Her husband had always known the truth about her faulty overconfidence and ego, but her daughter? It was a shocking revelation. "Was it all about the money?" Rose had wondered. "You set a *serial killer* free. How many other murderers have you let off so you could wear those shoes?"

Avery glanced at the tan interior of her BMW.

The leather was faded and old. The black dashboard had been removed and updated with her transreceiver, police scanner, and a computer for when she was on stakeouts. The car, bought at the height of her arrogance and fame, now served as a memory of her indulgent past, and a testament to her future.

"You won't die in vain," she swore to the memory of Jenna Prince. "I promise."

The walk to the house felt like forever. The sound of her shoes on the cement, birds, distant cars, and noises all made her more aware of herself, and what she intended to do. "I hate you," Constance had spit all those years ago. "You're the *devil*. You're worse than the devil." "Get out of our house!" Donald had cried. "You already killed our daughter. What more do you want? *Forgiveness*? Who can ever forgive someone as sick and depraved as you?"

Avery walked up the steps.

A phone call would have been inappropriate, even more so than an impromptu visit. They needed to see her face, her desperation. And she needed *them*.

She rang the doorbell.

A middle-aged female voice cried out: "Who is it?"

Footsteps moved closer.

The door opened.

Constance Prince was white, with an unnatural tan and cropped, bleached-blond hair. Although she rarely left the house except for chores or Mahjong with friends, she had on a mask of heavy make-up: blush, eyeliner, and red lipstick. Wrinkles lined her mouth and eyes. She wore a light sweater and red slacks. Golden bracelets clinked on her wrists. Jewels hung from golden threads on both ears.

A few blinks and she seemed to focus in on Avery. The welcoming air of her posture and appearance quickly faded. A breath was sucked in and she stepped back as if in shock.

Another voice called out.

"Who is it, honey?"

Without a word, Constance tried to shut the door.

"Please," Avery said. "I just need to ask a favor. I'll be gone before you know it."

A sliver of Constance's face could be seen between the door and frame. Head low, she stood unmoving for a moment.

"Please," Avery begged. "I need something, but I can't do it without your approval."

"What do you want?" Constance whispered.

Avery searched the porch and street before she turned back to the door.

"Have you read the papers?"

"Yes."

"There's another killer on the loose. He's a lot like, the last one," Avery said without mentioning Howard Randall, "smart and hard to track. Another body was found, today. That makes two so far, but he might work in threes, which means another body isn't far off. I'm a cop now," she added. "That life, who I was back then, that's not who I am now. I'm trying to make amends. I'm trying to be *different*."

The door opened.

Donald Prince had replaced his wife. Older, extremely large and out of shape, he had short gray hair, reddish skin, and a look that spoke to his shock and fury. He wore a dirty T-shirt, shorts, and green clogs. A dirt-covered glove was over one of his hands.

"What the hell do you want?" he said. "Why are you here?" He looked down the street. "You're not welcome in this house. Haven't you done enough to our family?"

"I came to get your permission," she said.

"Permission?" he spit and almost laughed. "You don't need our permission for anything. *We want you out of our lives!* You killed our daughter. Don't you understand that?"

"I never killed your daughter."

His eyes widened.

"You think that *excuses* what you did?"

"What I did was wrong," she said, "and I have to live with that—every day. I'm different now. I'm a cop. I try to *right* these wrongs, not allow them to go free."

85

"Well, good for you." He aggressively nodded. "Too little, too late for us, though. Isn't it?"

He tried to close the door.

"*Wait*," Avery said.

She held a palm on the painted wood.

"There's a new killer. Just like Howard Randall. Right in our backyard. He'll kill again. I'm sure of it. And soon. My leads are cold. I need a fresh perspective. I need to go visit Howard, see if he can help. I want your permission."

A laugh came from inside.

The door opened.

Donald leaned back, impervious.

"You want my permission?" he said. "To talk to the killer of my daughter, so you can stop another killer?"

"That's right."

"Sure," he said with a fake smile. "Good luck."

Any familiarity left his face, and a dark, murderous glare penetrated Avery.

"I don't care *who* you are now. You hear me? You come to my house again? You talk to my wife?" Violence burned in his eyes. His voice turned into a whisper. "I'll kill you," he swore. "And *that* will be justice. *True* justice."

CHAPTER EIGHTEEN

South Bay House of Corrections was a tremendous brown complex that spanned over six square blocks in the South End of Boston. The fortress was laid out in the shape of a triangle, with few windows and even fewer ways to enter. Multiple smaller buildings, high walls, and endless gates around the property made its entrance an enigma to the average visitor.

Avery had been to South Bay a few times before, both as an attorney and a cop. Even though it was easy for her to navigate Massachusetts Avenue to the number of side streets that needed to be utilized in order to park on Bradson Street and gain access to the main building, it was always a time-consuming and overly complicated process.

Visitors normally had to give written permission to enter at least a day in advance. If no advanced warning was given, they were usually turned away at the door for security reasons, regardless of their name, position, or excuse. The fact that Avery was a cop meant little to the overseers at South Bay. Prisons were like private islands, states unto themselves where employees were only accountable to their warden and the major.

Avery, however, wasn't a typical visitor.

A pseudo-celebrity at South Bay, she was known by nearly everyone on staff. The trial where she had Howard Randall acquitted of murder had been televised. What had *also* been televised was his bloody surrender only days later. During both ordeals, her face had been plastered everywhere, and until her disappearance and eventual reemergence in the Boston PD, her name had become synonymous with corrupt lawyers and a legal system in need of a massive overhaul.

At the metal detector, a guard shouted.

"Hey, Ms. Black. Check it out, Joey! Look who's here. Avery Black is back."

"What's up, Ms. Black?"

Avery offered a limp wave.

"Hi, guys."

She placed her items on the table and moved through the scanner.

Another guard bowed.

"To what do we owe this honor, Ms. Black?"

"I'm here to see Howard Randall."

"*Oh!*" a bunch of guards cooed.

"Wish I was a fly on *that* wall," someone said. "Careful, Black. Randall got moved to B-Block two months ago. He carved up an inmate pretty-bad. That old man can move!"

After the metal detectors, she was frisked and allowed to move into the visitors' room.

"Name?" said a chubby, dour woman inside a gated office.

"Avery Black. Homicide. Boston PD."

"I don't see you on our list, Black. You'll have to come back another time."

A passing guard made a face.

"Nah, nah," he said, "let her through. Do you know who this is? Avery Black. Got that crazy old geezer Randall off for murder. Most riveting case I ever watched."

"You'll take the heat?"

"Yeah, yeah. Give her a pass. I'll get someone down to Randall. See if he's up for a chat. Sorry, Ms. Black, but if Randall don't want to see you, there's nothing we can do."

"Understood," she said.

The caged waiting room was large and painted green. Buzzers continually resounded beyond the gates, along with slamming doors. Multiple tables and chairs were occupied by visitors waiting for their chance to see loved ones. A Mexican couple was fighting while their three children ran around and tried to talk to others.

What am I doing here? Avery wondered.

"Black! It's your lucky day," the guard called. "Randall said he's been expecting you. No public visiting room, though. He's got to stay caged. The moment he opens his mouth, he gets in trouble. I'll walk you downstairs and set you up outside his cell. More privacy for you too, right? And besides, you were his attorney once. Don't you have lawyer-client privileges?"

The walk down to the basement was everything Avery remembered.

Prisoners cried out and clanked on their cells. "Get me out of here! I'm innocent!" Guards screamed. "Shut or it's in the Box!" Whispers reached her, from passing guards to prisoners alike. "Hey, sweet thing. You want a private?"

The basement level was darker than the rest of the prison, with poor lighting and thick black doors against gray-painted concrete. White numbers were painted on each door. B1…B2…B3. The guard passed by every door and opened another gate.

"We put him in the conference room for you," he said. "You should be more comfortable there. When you're done just yell out."

One unmarked black door among many was opened.

Howard Randall sat at one end of a long metal table in an extremely narrow room. He had a large head with minimal, gray shaved hair on the sides. Thick glasses adorned his wrinkled face. Small eyes peered out at Avery with excitement. He was dressed in an orange jumpsuit. Withered hands were clasped on the table and kept in place by handcuffs. Similarly, his feet had been cuffed and latched to the table legs to prevent any real movement.

"Here you go, Howard," the guard said. "See what I do for you? They didn't want to let her down. She didn't call first. But *I* got her in. That's got to be worth something, right?"

Howard gave him a smile and a thankful nod.

"Of course, Officer Roberts," he said in a soft-spoken, confident voice. "Why don't we talk about payment later?"

The beefy, stubble-faced guard smiled back. "Good deal," he said. "Remember," he reminded Avery, "just holler when you're done. I'll be right outside. Don't carve her up now Howard," he laughed.

The door slammed shut.

The last time Avery had seen him was three years earlier, an uneventful trip she hoped would give her some answers. All Howard had done was talk about how thankful she should have been, for all he'd given her.

He appeared meeker than he had during her last visit. Poor food and no exercise, Avery thought. But his eyes...his eyes shone bright like stars.

"How are you, Howard?"

"How are *you*, Avery?"

"Always the therapist," she said. "What was that all about?" she asked with a look over her shoulder. "What kind of payment does he expect?"

"Officer Roberts likes to be fondled," he said. "He appreciates older men. I excite him. He'll want some private time later."

"I thought you were asexual?"

Howard offered a shrug.

"It gets lonely in here," he explained. "We do what we do to survive, don't we, Avery?"

She stiffened and squinted in defense.

"What's that supposed to mean?"

89

A lighter, more carefree air came to Howard. He attempted to open his palms and sit back and relax; the chains held him close to the table.

"Come now, Avery," he said, "why so guarded? You came to *me*. I'm a simple prisoner. How can I possibly hurt you any longer?"

"I heard you sliced up another inmate to get down here."

"That was different." He nodded in understanding. "My actions were completely warranted given the situation. Please, come. Sit down. Visits are so rare these days. Trust me. I won't bite," he said with a coy, sinister smile that exposed small teeth.

The sickness that Avery had felt toward him came back and hit her full force. She had the urge to wretch. He manipulated me, she thought, lied to me, set out to destroy my life. Why did I come here? Why would I trust him? He can't help me.

As he if he could read her mind, he said, "You came about the case, didn't you?"

"What case?"

"In today's paper, they're calling him the Sorority Killer, if I remember correctly. Two victims, both college students, unusually…placed, yes? Like mannequins."

"What do you know about it?"

"Sit, " he said again.

Reluctantly, Avery pulled the seat away from the table and sat down.

"That's better now, isn't it?" he cooed.

"The guard said you were expecting me."

"*Yes*," he said.

"How did you know I would come?"

"I didn't *know*, Avery. I'm not a mind-reader. But I do know things," he whispered and leaned forward. "I know you've recently been promoted to detective, homicide division, and that you're in charge of this case, yes? The papers say as much. And I know you have one great skill, Avery, and that is your tenacity of will. You'll stop at nothing to *win*. But you're a little out of your league on this one, aren't you? Defending the common man is one thing. Hunting down gang members is another; those people have basic needs and desires, and easy motives to understand. But people like me?" He let the words hang in the air. "We're a very different breed. Our motives, our *purpose* is often harder to perceive by…lesser mortals."

"Are you calling me a lesser mortal?"

He tipped his head as if to say "yes" without acknowledging the fact.

"I know you're *here*," he said, "which means you must need something. I'm guessing you want me to help you solve this case. A bold move, Ms. Black. I thought you despised me, and yet here you are, coming to me for aid. We're *partners*, again."

"We were never been partners."

"We've *always* been partners," he instantly corrected. "I came to this place for *you*, Avery, to show you the light, to change you—not your clothes but who you are on the inside. One person, one life, can change the world, and you are proof—my greatest gift to humanity. You're different now. I can see it. The cocky swagger is gone. The pretentious air has been vanquished. You sit before me a humble servant of justice, not wealth or power or greed. I *like* this new you, Avery. I wholeheartedly *approve*."

The person he was talking about, the person he seemingly loved, was a shell of the woman Avery felt she'd been, a damaged, struggling shell that had fallen so far she almost never combed her hair or thought about what she might wear from day to day. She was a ghost, a ghost that drove around in her old car and dressed in clothes from her old life but was completely dead except for her strength of will, a will that forced her to seek out justice wherever she could so that one day, she might right the wrongs of her past and be set free.

"I hate who I've become," she said.

"And if you could go back," he wondered, "would you?"

No, Avery thought. She would never go back. That life was over. But this new life…it wasn't yet complete. She was still disgraced, still fighting from the shadows. Memories of her dark, empty apartment returned, of her life without friends or family—a daughter that wanted nothing to do with her. Suddenly, Avery felt herself slipping off a mental ledge, to a place she'd been only once before, a dark place.

"I can never go back," she said.

"So," Howard realized, "the past is gone, but the future is not yet bright. I can help you Avery. I *want* to help you."

Avery looked up, back in the room again, sitting before Howard Randall and immersed in a case that already seemed cold.

"I *need* your help," she admitted.

"And I need something from *you*, Avery."

His small brown eyes opened wide with passionate intensity, and he leaned forward as far as he could go and repeated: "I need something from *you*."

"What do you need?" she asked.

Randall's entire persona changed. Hands slapped on the table and he leaned forward and practically yelled in her face with intense, rapid-fire words.

"*Father*," he said, "Grover Black. Alcoholic. Rapist. Beater. Molester. *Murderer*."

The words, like shots to her heart, launched Avery back to the past and she was there again, with her father and mother in that house in Ohio.

"No," she declared.

"*Mother*. Layla Black. Alcoholic. Drug addict. *Insane!*"

Avery had been to therapists, lots of therapists, after the incident with Randall, but it was nothing like this. She'd been guarded then, in control the whole time. Now, Randall had reduced her to a six-year-old child with only a few words and incredible passion.

Tears came, the instinctual tears of a young girl that wanted to save her mother from a gun-toting father that knew no bounds.

"*Father!* Alcoholic. Shamer. *Murderer!*"

Desperate, out of her head, Avery stood up and banged on the door.

"*Let me out*," she called.

Randall closed his mouth. He leaned back and raised a brow.

"Your killer is an artist, yes?" he said. "The bodies are positioned like lovers? He's an introvert, a dreamer. Not someone that would pick girls randomly off the street. He has to find them, watch them, know them from *somewhere*. Think, Avery. Think…"

The guard opened the door.

Avery rushed out.

CHAPTER NINETEEN

Avery sat hunched over the wheel of her car, still in the prison parking lot, destroyed, a mess, a husk, tears streaming down her face. Horrible sobs broke free from her throat. At one point, she jerked up and screamed and slammed the wheel.

Words.

Every time she heard one of his words, she cried harder.

Molester. Alcoholic. *Murderer.*

"No, no, no."

She banged her head to get the images out: her father in the woods, gun in hand. The body behind him. Varicose veins. Gray hair. That green dress.

"*Get out, get, out, get out,*" Avery begged.

She'd almost forgotten until then. So many years had been spent trying to forget the past, to get out of Ohio and wipe away her terrible history. In only a few words, Howard Randall had brought it all back.

You're just like them, she cried in misery.

Murderer.

Alcoholic.

Just like them...just like them.

No! She mentally rallied. You're nothing like them! You're no murderer or drug addict. You're not sick in the head. You do your best every day. Mistakes? Sure, but you try your hardest, all the time.

Get him out of my head.

Get him out of my head.

Fists rubbed away her tears.

Sobs were stifled.

Pull yourself together, she commanded.

Tears came again, only this time, they were softer, gentler—not about her old, painful past, but her new life, her lonely, tormented existence.

She hit the wheel.

"*Pull it together!*"

A detailed clarity came to her in that moment. Everything felt sharp and focused: the border of the windshield, her arm, the cars parked around her, the sky. Not exactly herself but fully in control, Avery picked up her phone to call Finley.

"Yo, yo," he answered.

93

"Finley," she said, "where are you?"

"I'm in the office working my ass off. Where the hell are *you*? I should get a raise for this, you know? Aren't I supposed to get the day off for finding a psycho? I just had one of the greatest chases of my life and now I'm stuck in an office. I should be out there having a beer."

His entire monologue had come out like a single word.

Avery rubbed her eyes.

"Finley, *slow down*. What have you found so far?"

"Why are people always telling me to slow down?" he complained as if he were truly upset. "I talk just fine. Everyone in my crew understands me perfectly. Maybe *other* people are the problem, ever think about that? My mother used to say."

"Finley! The update."

"The body is with the coroner," he said, calmer and slower. "Crime scene wrapped up. They found some fibers but it looks like they're the same ones from Jenkins: cat hair, a few dabs of plant extract on her clothes. Last few hours I've been looking for connections, like you asked. Different majors: economics and accounting. One a junior, one a senior. Different sororities, no family connections at all. Blah, blah, blah. Talked to Ramirez. He said Cindy's parents mentioned an art class she took in Cambridge last semester. Place called Art for Life. Located on Cambridge Street and Seventh. Called Tabitha's friends for a connection. Waiting to hear back."

Artist, Avery thought. He said our killer is an artist.

"Who teaches there?" she asked. "Who owns the studio?"

"How the fuck should I know?" Do I have a thousand hands, now?" he barked. "You gave me like, a hundred jobs. I have no idea who teaches that fuckin' class. I told you, I'm waiting to hear back."

She closed her eyes.

"OK," she said. "Thanks."

"You coming back to help me out or what?" Finley complained.

"I need to tie up some loose ends," she said. "You have Cindy's address? And Tabitha's? I want to swing by their dorms and see what I can find."

"I was already at Tabitha's dorm. Just some chick room. Fancy clothing and stupid posters. Nothing there."

"Let *me* be the judge of that."

Cindy had lived in a house not far from the Kappa Kappa Gamma suite, or from her boyfriend. The two-story white Tudor with blue trim housed two people. Cindy rented out the first floor; the second floor was inhabited by another Harvard senior.

Avery called ahead to ensure Harvard officials would let her inside.

A spare set of keys was under a rock by the front porch.

Cindy's apartment smelled like stale air. There were four main rooms: living room, bedroom, a spare room she'd converted into an office, and the kitchen. A few pieces of modern art adorned the walls.

The office was filled with a slew of library-issued texts, along with a number of paperback romances. Papers were stacked on the desk.

Avery checked through the files. Medical bills, class folders, job interview letters, resumes. Everything was neat and orderly. Avery took notes on her phone: Cindy's medical provider, every teacher she'd had, the places she'd interviewed, and her current employer: Devante Accounting Firm. The letter of her acceptance as a junior accountant in their firm was proudly displayed on the desk.

No mention of the art class could be found, but there was a framed, hand-painted picture on the wall that had Cindy's signature at the bottom. The image was a bowl of fruit. Avery turned the picture over. On the back was a stamp: Art for Life, their address, and the logo of a hand depicted as a paint palette. Avery put everything back the way she found it, headed outside, and hopped in her car.

MIT was called ahead to ensure they would allow her into Tabitha's room. The dean's assistant said he would take care of everything.

As soon as she hung up, Avery's phone rang.

"It's Jones," came a Jamaican voice.

"Tell me something," Avery said.

"Nothing out here, man. The cabin is empty."

"What the hell have you been doing all day?"

"*Research*, man," Jones complained, "investigating. Took a while to get up here. Had to get the keys, right? Then Thompson wanted to drive and he has absolutely *no* sense of direction. GPS got us all screwy. But," he admitted with another swig of his beer,

95

"we got here and turned the place over. Nothing. You sure the kid stayed here?"

"You wasted a whole day," Avery said.

"You're not *listening*, Black! We been working hard."

"Two girls are dead," Avery said. "Or maybe you forgot that? We've got a serial killer on the loose and you're jerking around in a lakeside cabin. Get back on Cambridge surveillance. And *this* time," she snapped, "I want a detailed report on my desk by tomorrow afternoon. I want to know *exactly* how you spent every hour. You hear me?"

"*Aw, come on!* Black. I'm *begging* you," Jones cried. "That job is crazy. Ain't no way to track a car for miles and miles like that. It's *impossible*. I need like, ten other people."

"Take Thompson."

"*Thompson?*" Jones laughed. "He's worse than Finley."

"Remember," Avery emphasized. "A detailed report on my desk tomorrow afternoon. Make sure Thompson understands. Screw this up and I call Connelly."

She hung up.

How am I supposed to do anything in Homicide if half my team won't even respect my authority? she fumed.

By the time she reached her next destination, the sky was dark.

Tabitha had lived in the heart of the MIT, just off Vassar Street. Her roommate answered the door; she was a small, mousy girl with long black hair, glasses, and a face covered in pimples. The room was large: a main living area, open kitchen, and two bedrooms.

"Hi," the girl said, "you must be Avery."

"Yeah, thanks for letting me in."

"That's her room, there," she pointed.

The girl appeared dour and miserable.

"Were you two friends?" Avery wondered.

"Not really," she said and walked away. "Tabitha was popular."

Tabitha's room was extremely cluttered.

The filing cabinet was more of a place to cram loose papers. A quick search uncovered everything from receipts to a resume and a smelly sandwich wrapper. The most revealing item was the number of pictures that lined the walls, all seemingly done by Tabitha herself: farm scenes, the MIT skyline, a bowl of fruit.

Avery looked at the back of one of the framed paintings.

A stamp read: Art for Life.

CHAPTER TENTY

Molly Green was having a rough night. She puffed a lock of blond hair out of her face, wiped her brow, and pretended to roll up her sleeves.

"Luke and Gidget!" she cried. "I've had just about enough of this!"

The house where she worked as a part-time nanny appeared large and empty. She stood in the oversized living room on the first floor and searched behind couches. Face against the sliding glass doors that led to the back porch, she cupped her eyes from the interior light and thought: They *better* not be out there.

No one was in the kitchen, closets, or downstairs bathroom.

A small side guest room was equally vacant.

"I'm serious," she called, "it's *way* past your bedtime."

She stomped up the stairs in high heels, a black leather skirt, and the skimpy tank top she planned to wear to the party later that night.

"You better be in bed!"

Sure enough, both Luke and Gidget were hidden under the covers and giggling like mad because they'd once again outsmarted her.

The kids shared the single room and each had their own bed. A stark contrast could be seen between Gidget's side of the room and Luke's. Hers had actually been painted pink; it was neat and orderly, with toys in their proper place and clothes in their drawers. Luke's side of the room was painted dark blue. All of his toys were on the floor, clothing thrown everywhere, and the walls were smudged with dirt and markers.

"Now I see how it is," Molly said. "Make me run all over the house and then pretend you were asleep all this time. Nice try."

The covers were thrown off and both of them vied for her attention.

"Read me a book, Molly."

"Don't turn off the hall light," Luke said.

"Your parents will kill me if they find you up when they get back. You *have* to go to bed. No more books. I'll leave the hall light on. You hear me? I find either of you roaming the halls again or trying to scare me downstairs, I become a squealer. And you know what that means."

"*No, no,*" Gidget cried.

97

"Don't tell Dad," Luke pleaded.

"All right then. Bedtime. Good night."

Once again, she shut the door, leaving it open about a quarter of an inch so they could see the hall light.

Back downstairs she thought: *Ugh...Kids.*

A quick look in the living room mirror confirmed that she still looked *amazing*—green eye shadow in place, lashes long, lipstick perfect, blue eyes sparkling.

You look *hot*, she thought with a squeal.

About twenty minutes later, as Molly was watching a taped edition of *The John Oliver Show*, Mr. and Ms. Hachette silently opened the front door.

Pleasantries were given all around.

Molly updated them on her night. "Dinner was great. Books were read. I gave them both baths. We ran around for a while and they went to bed. Nothing special."

As always, the Hachettes asked if she wanted to say any longer, eat something, or just crash in the guest room. Molly declined.

All she could think about was the party, a huge Brandeis bash given by one of the biggest fraternities on campus. Three boys that she'd been seeing would all be there, but none of them were actually considered boyfriend material. Tonight, she was hoping to find someone new.

She grabbed her bag and skipped out the door.

Let the games begin, she thought, smiling.

* * *

He had been waiting outside for a while, hidden in the shadows of his minivan interior. For the last hour, he'd been there, watching and preparing for the right moment. He'd silently watched as Molly had searched the house for the kids and found them in bed. He'd seen the Hachettes enter the house.

He was parked on a very quiet street in a tree-lined neighborhood just northeast of Brandeis University, only a few minutes' drive to the college and about a twenty-minute walk. Molly, he knew, would choose to walk. She would hop down the stairs, make a left onto Cabot Street, and then a right onto Andrea Road. After that, she usually altered her route based on where she needed to be on campus.

As he suspected, Molly skipped down the house steps and turned left.

He silently exited his minivan and moved to the back, where he pretended to be unloading something from the trunk space. He loudly shut the trunk, sighed, and stepped onto the street. Molly was headed directly toward him. He took off his cap and looked up.

Immersed in her own thoughts, Molly nearly bumped right into him. "Oh, sorry," she mumbled.

"That's fine," he replied.

"Hey!" She suddenly brightened. "I *know* you. How are you?"

"I'm all right." He smiled. "Having a bit of car trouble here. Wait a minute." He frowned and rubbed his chin. "I thought you lived somewhere on the Brandeis campus?"

"Yeah, I do," she acknowledged, "I just work here. See that house," and she turned to point it out, "I nanny for their kids during the week. But don't worry, I..."

The moment she swiveled, he quickly punctured her with his needle.

"*Hey!* Ow! What the..."

Molly began to fall. He slid behind her to catch.

"Are you all right?" He pretended to panic. "Molly?" He tapped her cheeks in mock concern. "Molly, are you OK?" He scanned the area.

The streets were dark and empty.

"Don't worry," he whispered, "*I'll* take care of you."

CHAPTER TWENTY ONE

Large glass windows buttressed both sides of the glass door of Art for Life Studios. Avery could see a narrow, packed gallery space inside with all kinds of modern art: sculptures, paintings, drawings, and retro collages. Further back, the room opened up into a much larger area, with a circle of easels for what she assumed was the art class meeting area.

Her phone rang.

"Black," she answered.

"Who's your boy?" Finley said. "I just got a call back from one of Tabitha's friends. The victim definitely took an art class at that studio."

"I already figured it out. Didn't you notice all the art when you were in her dorm?"

"What art?"

"In her *room*."

"That wasn't *art*." Finley blanched. "That was *garbage*. I thought she bought it at a yard sale. Look, Black, don't bust my balls. I just got you a good lead."

"I'm here now," she said. "The studio is closed."

"I'm at a bar," he replied. "My shift ended two hours ago. I'd invite you down here, but I don't think they let lesbians in this place."

"I'm *not* a lesbian," she said.

"Really? Could have fooled me."

"You're a disgusting human being, you know that, Finley?"

"Nah, nah," he said, "I'm a good guy. Just my upbringing. It was all messed up. I'll do better next time. I promise. You're cool, even if you're a lesbian. Seriously. I got your back. See you in the morning. I gotta go get fucked up."

Too hyped up on adrenaline to relax or sleep, Avery headed home to investigate Art for Life in the comfort of her living room. On the way, she ordered takeout Chinese.

The apartment was kept dim. A single lamp was turned on by the couch. She sat at the table in the living room and chowed down on food while she worked.

Art for Life had been in business for over five years. The owner was a man named Wilson Kyle, a former artist and businessman who also owned a restaurant near the studio and two

100

buildings near the area. A quick search on her police database turned up nothing on Kyle.

Two people were employed at his studio: a full-time salesman named John Lang and a part-time female employee who came in on the weekends. Kyle himself taught the art classes on Wednesday and Thursday nights, but Lang taught two classes on alternate Saturdays.

Lang had a record.

A registered sex offender, with two incidents filed from seven years ago. One was from a boy he apparently babysat, and the other was from a girl who had lived on his block. Both sets of parents said their children had been molested. Lang pleaded not guilty but then flipped his plea to avoid a trial and possible jail time. He was given five years probation, mandatory counseling for a year, and a stigma that would remain with him for life.

According to the police files, his height and weight matched the estimates for the killer.

Avery sat back.

It was close to midnight. She was wide awake and ready to bang down the door of John Lang. This could be the guy, she thought.

High from the possibility of catching the killer, Avery wanted to share the good news with someone. Strangely, Ray Henley came to mind, but the thought of an awkward, late-night call with someone she'd only recently met was too daunting to face. Finley was out of the question, and the captain had given specific orders about disturbing him at home.

She thought about calling her daughter.

The last time they'd spoken was months earlier, and it had not gone well.

Avery sent her an email instead. "Hey," she wrote, "been thinking about you a lot lately. Would love to talk in person. How about lunch this weekend. Maybe Saturday? Our usual place? Noon? Let me know. I love you. Mom."

Still eager to talk to someone, she dialed the hospital.

The phone rang numerous times before a sleepy voice picked up.

"Hello?"

"Ramirez," she said, "how you doing?"

"Damn, Black. What time is it?"

"Almost one."

"This better be good," he mumbled, "I was in the middle of a great dream. I was in a boat on a clear blue ocean, and this mermaid comes up to me and we start making out."

"Wow," she said, but she wasn't in the mood to listen to him describe his sex dreams.

"I've got a good lead," she went on, "Art for Life. Guy that works there is named John Lang. Has a sheet. Both girls took classes there. Could be our guy."

"I thought Finley had already solved your case," Ramirez joked. "He said he took down a genuine serial killer yesterday."

"Finley wouldn't know a serial killer from a *box* of cereal."

Ramirez laughed.

"He's crazy, right? Heard about the old man with the dead bodies in his basement. Wild shit. I guess some people. You just never know."

"How are you feeling?"

"Better, better. I really just want to get the hell out of here and back to work."

"I know, but you need to rest."

"Yeah, yeah, and it's not that bad really," he said. "I got a private room, nice bed, paid leave, decent food. *You're* the one I'm worried about. I mean, Finley? Cap must be out for you."

"I don't know, I'm coming around. Take away the bigotry and racism and that foul mouth of his, and he's actually not that bad. I just wish I could understand him."

A laugh was instantly cut short.

"Ah man, that hurt," Ramirez groaned. "Gotta be careful. Stitches are killing me. Yeah, he's hardcore," he said. "Irish from the south side. He used to be a D-Boy. Did you know that? They nearly killed him when he switched sides. You see all his tats? He's got a full body."

"No. I haven't seen his full-body tats yet."

Ramirez snorted.

"Well, look, Avery, thanks for the call. I feel a little tired so I'm going to go. Good luck with this new lead. I'll be praying for you."

Avery grabbed a beer and moved out onto the balcony. Fast-moving clouds were scattered across a moonlit sky.

She took a long swig.

I got you, she thought.

CHAPTER TWENTY TWO

Avery took two pills to sleep that night and set the alarm for seven; Art for Life didn't open until nine, but she wanted to be ready.

At six forty-five she awoke on her own, groggy and eager to start the day. She dressed in her usual attire and just swapped out the colors: brown slacks and a blue button-down shirt. Blue is calming, she thought. I want everyone to be calm today. The walkie-talkie was hitched to the back of her belt. Gun was locked in its holster. Badge was visible near her buckle.

She glanced in the mirror.

According to most people, she still looked like a knockout. However, flaws were all Avery could see: lines that hadn't been there a few years ago, the weighed worry in her eyes, hair made unhealthy by so many bleachings.

With a pouty face, a dancing twirl, and a pucker of her lips, Avery smiled.

That's the girl I know, she thought.

Cambridge Street only had light traffic that early in the morning. Avery stopped for coffee and a bagel, and then parked her car on the opposite side of the street from the studio, about two doors down. The wait was the most annoying part of the job, and Avery settled in for the long stretch.

Surprisingly, John Lang appeared in Avery's rearview mirror at close to eight thirty.

He was lean and tall, not exactly a perfect body match to the killer, but it was her only lead, and there was a connection, and the way he walked reminded her of the killer: with a flair in his steps, all hips and hard feet.

When he reached the office, Lang unlocked the door.

Avery exited her car.

"Excuse me," she called from across the street. "Can I have a word?"

Lang had an unpleasant face, thinning blond hair, and glasses. A frown wrinkled his brow as he watched Avery for a moment and then headed inside.

"Hey!" Avery yelled. "Police."

She flashed her badge.

Surprise and worry overcame John Lang. He tentatively peeked out the windows. Across the street, two people with coffee watched

Avery jog to the studio. Resigned, Lang took on an imperious air and opened the door.

"The shop is currently closed," he said.

"I'm not here about art."

"What can I help you with, Officer?"

"I'd like to talk about Cindy Jenkins and Tabitha Mitchell."

A befuddled look crossed his face.

"Those names mean nothing to me."

"Are you sure? Because both of those girls took art classes at this studio, and now they're both dead. Maybe you'd like to revise that statement? Can I come inside?"

During a long pause, Lang peered into the studio, at his computer, and then again out toward the street.

"Yes," he said, "but only for a minute. I'm very busy."

The studio was cool as if an air conditioner had been timed to turn on early. Lang dropped a bag on his desk, sat in a large black swivel chair, and turned to Avery. No seat was offered for her. A couple of cushioned stools were scattered around the space. Avery stood.

"Cindy Jenkins and Tabitha Mitchell," she said.

"I told you, I don't know them."

"They took classes here."

"A lot of people take classes here. Can I get a time period?"

"Why don't you look them up on your computer?"

He flushed red.

"Those files are routinely purged," he said.

"Really? You don't keep client names and addresses so you can send fliers and emails? I find that hard to believe."

"We keep the names and addresses," he said. "But the documents that we use when they first arrive for classes are destroyed, so I wouldn't be able to give you a time period."

"You're lying," she said.

"Am I being charged with something?" he demanded.

"Have you committed a crime?"

"Absolutely not!"

Avery wasn't convinced. There was something about the way he said the words, and the drift of his gaze, and the computer he refused to turn on.

"How long have you worked here?" she asked.

"Five years."

"Who hired you?"

"Wilson Kyle."

"Does Wilson Kyle know you're a registered sex offender?"

Shame blushed on Lang's cheeks, and the beginning of tears. He sat taller in his chair and glared at her with malice.

"Yes," he said, "he does."

"Where were you on Saturday night? And on Wednesday night?"

"Home. I watch movies."

"Can anyone vouch for that?"

On the verge of a breakdown, Lang practically shook from anger.

"How dare you," he hissed. "What are you trying to do? I've made amends for my past. I went to jail and had to seek out professional help and perform community service and have a red flag waved around for the rest of my life: 'Sex Offender.' I'm better now," he swore as his body relaxed and the tears began to fall. "I'm different. All I ask is that you people just leave me alone."

He was hiding something. Avery could feel it.

"Did you kill Cindy Jenkins and Tabitha Mitchell?"

"No!"

"Show me that computer."

A scrunched face and a shake of his head told Avery all she needed to know.

"If you won't log on and let me look at your search history right now, I'll be back this afternoon with a warrant for your arrest."

"*What's going on here?*" someone roared.

A large, extravagant man stood in the doorway. He had perfectly cut, flowing white hair combed back from his face and a trimmed white goatee. Small, chunky black glasses framed angry green eyes. A crimson summer sweater was twirled over a white T-shirt. He wore jeans and black Crocs.

Lang covered his face and instantly fell apart.

"I'm sorry! *I'm so sorry.*"

Avery flashed her badge.

"And you would be?"

"Wilson Kyle. I own this establishment."

"My name is Avery Black. Homicide. Boston PD. I have reason to believe Mr. Lang here might be implicated in two possible homicides."

He raised his brows in disbelief.

"*John* Lang?" he said. "You mean *him*? The man cowering before you? You think *he* could be responsible for murder?"

105

"Two girls from two different colleges," she said and scrutinized every movement of John Lang, "positioned: one in the park and one in a cemetery."

"I've read about this case," Kyle confirmed.

A large palm went on John's shoulder.

"John?" he asked with a sensitive tone. "Do you know anything about this?"

"*I don't know anything!*" John cried. "Haven't I been through enough?"

"How exactly have you implicated him in these crimes?"

"Those two girls both came here. He has a record. He has no alibi for the nights of the abductions and he won't let me see what's on that computer," she said.

"Do you have a warrant?"

"No, but I can get one."

Wilson Kyle lowered down with his immense presence and, with incredible patience and empathy, he tried to get John to hold his gaze.

"John," he said, "it's all right. The police are trying to solve a crime. What's on the computer that you don't want her to see? You can be honest with me."

"*I had to look!*" he sobbed.

"It's all right, John," he said and leaned forward to whisper, "I won't judge you."

He rubbed John's back, helped him up, and logged onto the computer.

"Password?" he asked.

John sniffled and rubbed his nose. A shake of his head and a soft, barely perceptible reply was whispered.

Wilson Kyle typed in his password.

"There you are, Officer Black," he said. "Look and see. Come, John," he added. "Let's wait over here. It's going to be all right. I promise. The officer just wants to confirm you're not involved in a mass murder. You're no murderer, are you, my boy? No, of course not, John. Of course not."

Avery sat at the desk.

A quick search of the history revealed nothing. Art sites. Scrabble Word help and multiple artists and their works. She went through each day. On Tuesday, early in the morning, she saw a slew of pornography sites.

She looked up.

John was seated in a chair, his head down, hands in his face. Wilson Kyle stood behind him and glared at Avery like a great lord being forced to watch something unthinkable, and that fact made him angrier and angrier.

Back to the computer, Avery clicked on a few of the links. Young children appeared, naked or half naked. Ages ranged from six to twelve. Utterly disgusted by what she saw, Avery clicked on other sites to try to make some rational argument as to why she should ignore what she found. Based on his proclivity for little children, it was hard for her to imagine him as the killer.

"Do you know where he was on Saturday night?" she asked.

"I do," Wilson said. "John was home watching a movie called *Night of the Hunter*. I know this because I recommended the movie, and he called me afterwards, I believe around ten o'clock, to express his feelings. I was unavailable, but I'm sure you can find that call if you check his phone records."

"Can you account for *your* actions this past week?" she asked Wilson.

Wilson laughed.

"Do you know who I am, Officer Black? No, of course not. Don't get me wrong. I'm not famous in any way, or especially well connected, but I have a deep interest in my community, and if I'm not out with friends, I'm usually feeding the homeless or at a charity auction somewhere in town. So, to answer your question: Yes. I *can* account for my actions all *month*, but I'm afraid I'll require a warrant before this can go any further."

You were wrong, Avery thought. This isn't your guy. She could see right through these people. John was sick, and Wilson was a pompous, self-righteous prick. But they weren't serial killers. They were too weak, both of them.

She sighed. She was wasting her time here.

She'd been in this place before—alone, no leads, out on a limb and bending the rules of her profession—but this time it felt personal. This time, it was about a serial killer. The last time Avery had dealt with a serial killer, she freed him and he killed again. Now it was as if that old case had been reborn again with this new killer, and if she could stop him somehow, she could free herself.

"I'll be in touch," Avery said and made her way out.

"Ms. Black," Wilson called.

"Yes?"

"I'll deal with the pornography you just found, have no doubt. I'm curious, though. Do you know *why* John might have searched

107

for those images? And do you know why he molested those children so long ago? Let me tell you so that you can get some perspective, and maybe you won't walk into another house or office space later on, half-cocked and full of prejudice and insinuation. You see, John here was raped repeatedly by his father *and* his mother as a child."

John sobbed softly in his hands.

Wilson held onto John's shoulders like a protective angel.

"I'm assuming you don't know what happens to children that are molested, Ms. Black. They learn that such behavior is normal, and expected. And as they get older, they become aroused by small children because that's what they were trained to do—become aroused. It's a sick, frightening cycle that is almost impossible to break, but John here has been trying very hard. Very hard indeed. This simple lapse," he said and pointed to the computer, "shouldn't erase how hard he's worked to reconstruct his past. If you knew anything at all about human nature, you might understand that."

"Thanks for the lesson," Avery said.

"And one more thing," Wilson added and walked toward her with his face red from withheld anger. "You had no right to come into this studio and interrogate *anyone* without proper authorization. The second you leave here, I'll be on the phone with your commanding officer, and anyone else I have to contact, and I'm going to recommend you be fired, or at the very least, suspended for your blatant disregard of the laws and some common human decency."

* * *

Avery was in a haze when she walked out of the studio.

Positive she'd found her killer only a few hours before, now she was almost certain John Lang was a dead end, and that she would face a lot of fury should Wilson Kyle call the office.

Embarrassed at her actions, she hopped into her car and drove.

The words of Howard Randall echoed in her mind: *Your killer is an artist...not someone that would pick girls randomly off the street....*

I followed your lead, she argued. I found a connection.

Randall's last words turned into a whisper.

He has to find them from somewhere...

Where? she fought. Where does he find them? There has to be another connection, something I missed.

There has to be something else, something I'm missing, another link.

The office was her de facto destination, but something kept telling her that any answers wouldn't come from the office. They would come from leads. She decided to assist Jones on the surveillance routes out of Cambridge. Thompson had already followed up on Graves. The cocky senior's alibi was solid: three friends confirmed his location on Saturday night.

She stopped off for another cup of coffee and some breakfast.

Her phone rang.

"Black," she said.

The voice on the other line sounded grim and unsatisfied.

"It's Connelly."

A shutter of worry passed through Avery. Did Wilson Kyle already call? Did we finally get a break on the case?

"What's up?" she said.

"You've having a real party out there, aren't you?" Connelly whispered.

"What's that supposed to mean?"

"This is getting out of control, Black. We look like a bunch of fucking idiots. *The cap is pissed.* And so am I, I *knew* you were all wrong for the job."

"What are you talking about?" she asked. "Did you just call to harass me?"

"You don't know?" he asked.

After a moment of silence, Connelly spoke again.

"Just got word from Belmont Police. They found a body over at the Children's Playground in Stony Brook Park. Sounds like our guy."

CHAPTER TWENTY THREE

Avery parked her car on the eastern edge of Stony Brook Park and walked down Mill Street to the entrance.

The Stony Brook Children's Playground was an expansive water park for children, combined with three separate playgrounds and a huge wooden fort, all nestled within a circle of trees and behind a fence near a gated community.

A number of Belmont police cruisers, along with news vans and reporters and crowds, surrounded the area by the gate.

"*There she is!*" someone shouted.

Before Avery could even think, a number of reporters made their way toward her. In her previous life, when she'd been fired from her law firm, Avery had assumed the cameras and lights and microphones would eventually fade away. Unfortunately, that had never been the case. She could always find herself as the butt of jokes in one paper or another on slow news days.

A small reporter with bobbed black hair shoved a mic in her face.

"Ms. Black," she said, "are you in a relationship with Howard Randall?"

"*What?*" Avery demanded.

Someone else extended a mic.

"You went to visit him yesterday. What did you two talk about?"

"Where are you getting this information?" Avery asked.

A paper was held out in front of her, and as Avery scanned the front page and turned to the news article inside, cameras were rolling, and everyone waited for a response.

The headline read "Two girls dead and no leads." The picture was from the cemetery. A sub-headline on the bottom said: "A Cop and A Killer: Romance Blooms." Avery saw herself sobbing inside her car, right beyond the prison walls.

The guards, she realized. They took pictures.

The actual news article was on the third page: "Who Runs The Boston PD?" Words like "incompetent," "mishandling," and "negligence" practically jumped off the page. One line: "Why would Boston PD allow a former attorney with questionable ethics to handle another possible serial killer case?"

Sick to her stomach, Avery handed the paper back.

"Can you give us a comment?" someone asked.

Avery pushed ahead in silence.

"Officer Black!? Officer Black!?"

A woman that couldn't have been more than ninety pounds found her way to Avery and punched her in the chest.

"You fucking piece of shit!" she cried. "My tax money pays for *you*? No way! I'm going to have you fired—you murdering son of a bitch."

The crowd moved in.

"*Why are you on this case?*" someone else shouted.

"Don't let her near kids!"

At the gate, Avery flashed her badge and an officer pushed her through.

"Who's in charge here?" she said.

"Right over there," the cop pointed. "Talbot Diggins. Lieutenant Diggins."

Normally, the abuse was easy for Avery to ignore, but today, after her dismal interrogation of John Lang and another dead body, and no leads, and the paper, and everything else, it took all of her energy just to stand tall and walk forward.

Even separated from the mob beyond the gate, she could hear people voicing their outrage as reporters pushed cameras through the bars.

Cops around the area turned and watched Avery pass. Some muttered under their breath. Others just looked at her with scorn.

When will it end? she wondered.

Talbot Diggins was an extremely large black man with a shaved head. He wore sunglasses and was sweating hard in the early morning heat. He was dressed in a slick gray suit and a T-shirt underneath, and the only items that gave him away as a cop were the badge around his neck and gun peeking out from the back of his jacket.

He noticed her and pointed.

"You Black?" he said.

"Yeah."

"Follow me."

The actual park was ignored. Behind the wide pool that normally sprayed water in countless directions, they passed a playground for toddlers and headed directly toward a wooden castle, complete with bridges, a moat, and a wooden city.

Lights from a police photographer flashed inside the wooden structure.

"Kid found her this morning," Talbot said. "Ten-year-old girl. Said she was trying to play with her but the body wouldn't move. So she touched her. Cold as ice."

The wooden structure had an opening at its front that served as a castle entrance.

A dead girl sat in the entrance, positioned as if she'd simply taken a break from play. She was eighteen or nineteen, Avery guessed. Blond hair. Dressed in a tight-fitting shirt and skirt. A whimsical, humorous expression lined her face. Hands were up and had been bound to a bar over her head with very fine fiber, like fishing line. The eyes themselves, like the others Avery had seen, appeared drugged and tortured.

"Do you know who she is?" Avery asked.

"Not yet."

A quick look and Avery could tell the victim wore all her undergarments. Maybe that last girl was a fluke? she wondered

Like the other girls, this one appeared to be looking at something. Avery tracked the line of sight to the toddler playground. Immediately, she knew what the victim had been meant to see: a painted mural of children that lined one of the plastic borders. The children were boys and girls, multicultured, and there were a lot of them, all holding hands.

Talbot eyed her suspiciously.

"Is it true?" he asked.

"Is what true?"

"You and Randall. Papers say you two are an item. Is it true?"

"That's disgusting," she said.

"Maybe," he offered. "But is it *true*?"

"None of your business," she said.

"Man, you really screwing up my day, you know that? First, I have to deal with some serial killer fallout because you can't do your job, and now you won't even answer a simple question. Come on, we've got a big office pool riding on this."

"You don't have to worry about this," Avery said. "My department will—"

"*Nah, nah, nah,*" he complained, "that's not going to happen. This is *my* crime scene, you understand? I called your department out of courtesy. *I can't give you this,*" he declared and indicated the dead body. "You already have two dead girls in under a week. Now we've got a third in Belmont. You know what that spells? Team up."

"We don't need to—"

"Oh, we *do* need to," he said with his eyes rolled back. "Honestly. How close are you to cracking this case?"

"We have a lot of solid leads that—"

"*Beep! Incorrect answer!*" he cried like an alarm and pretended to be a robot. "I don't believe that," he calmly indicated. "Look at you. You look as messed up as they say in the papers. And you won't even give a fellow cop a hint about your personal life. What's *that* all about? So you know what? We're teammates now, and in Belmont, we solve cases quick."

"Oh yeah?" Avery said. "How many bodies have you ever seen like this?"

"Pssss," he sang.

"No, I'm serious."

"*That don't matter.*"

"I'll tell you what matters," she said. "I've been on the case for under a week and I know the general area where the killer lives. I know his height and a description of his body. I know he has a soft spot for pets and what he drives, and from the looks of this third body?" she said and pointed to the dead girl, "I know he's not finished yet. Three used to be his magic number. Now that's changed. I know a lot of other things," she spit. "But you know what? You're right. This is your jurisdiction. *Figure it out for yourself.*"

She spun around to walk out.

"*Whoa, whoa, whoa,*" Talbot howled. "Hold on there, white lion!"

Talbot had a completely different demeanor when Avery looked back. His arms were open wide and he displayed a stunning smile with large white teeth.

"Here I thought I was dealing with a kitty cat, but what I really got is a white lion."

He sidled up to Avery, who was about an inch shorter and smaller in every way.

"I can't come between a lead detective and possible serial killer on a major case like this," he said. "Shit is all over the news. I *gotta* help you, whether I like it or not. Take your time," he said and waved around. "Check things out."

"But you just said—"

"*Nobody likes you,*" he emphasized in earnest. "My people can't think we're buddies. Hard enough being a black man out here. How about this: I'll have my people take care of this crime scene. We'll get the body to our coroner, try to figure out who she is and have forensics sweep the area. What's your number? Whisper it to me. Whisper..."

Avery whispered her number and Talbot made a nasty face, like he was taking down the digits of her supervisor so she could be reprimanded.

"I just called you," he said. "There it is... Now you have my number too. Once I hear back from everyone on my team. I'll send you a detailed report. Not happy? Talk to your captain, and have him call *my* captain, but I can tell you this already: this shit happened in *my* town this time, and that means Belmont police are involved. You wanna help me out? Share what you got?"

"Sure," she said, "we can do that. I'd also want my team to view the body and consult with your coroner."

"No problem."

"And I want complete access to this crime scene."

"You got it. We good?"

"Yeah," she said and frowned, "I think."

"*I don't give a shit* what *you think!*" Talbot yelled and backed up so everyone could hear. "*That's just the way it is, Black!*"

CHAPTER TWENTY FOUR

Talbot walked away right after his trash-talk to consult with his team. Most of the Belmont cops flashed nasty looks at Avery, or shook their heads. One of them could be heard saying, "Why do we have to share shit? This is a Belmont crime."

Avery took her time to walk around the area.

She stared at the body from multiple perspectives. Everyone ignored her, but every so often she could hear mothers screaming from beyond the gates, or hear reporters calling out questions.

A sense of the killer had begun to inhabit Avery. It had started in Lederman Park, and then at the cemetery, a feeling that she understood him somehow. He'd chosen quiet places, respectful places for dead. This one was different. Although the girl was placed in a park among trees and woods, it was a children's park, which had a more excitable energy than a cemetery or a bench near the river.

Why here? she wondered.

The visual of the girl, too, was different: she viewed multiple children, different genders and colors.

Something happened, she thought.

What changed?

Forensics and the coroner's report would be able to tell her if there were differences within the body or at the crime scene, but even if they found nothing, Avery was certain about her instincts. After working on cases involving killers for years—and *before* killers, on cases involving sleazy people in general as an attorney— she'd become an expert on subtle differences within people, and at crime scenes.

Alone, with no new leads, an abysmal morning and with protestors, parents, and Belmont police glaring at her like she was an unwanted guest, Avery put her head down and headed back to the car.

Her arrival at the A1 office was the perfect topping for a terrible day. The moment the elevator doors opened and Avery was seen, the entire office went silent. Sneers were on their faces. Jones shook his head and looked away and Thompson turned his back on her. Not a single nasty joke or laugh only made it worse.

Finley was at his desk. Slightly more empathetic than the rest of his department, he offered a sympathetic glance and lowered his head.

The morning paper, with her scandalous article about the visit with Howard Randall, was on a number of desks, and a few computer screens showed a similar picture of Avery, crying in her car outside the prison.

"Black," someone called, "get in here."

O'Malley waved from his office.

Connelly stood up.

"No. No," O'Malley pointed. "Not you. Just Black."

"This is my case," Connelly argued.

"If you want to keep it that way, you'll sit down and shut up."

Connelly stood defiantly and pushed out his chest.

"Am I in trouble?" Avery asked.

"Come on in." O'Malley waved and closed the door behind him. "What makes you think you're in trouble, Black? You tell me."

"I don't know," she said. "I went to see Howard Randall for a lead. He gave me one, well, not a good one, but a connection between those girls. He knew something."

A deep sigh came from O'Malley.

"What could Howard Randall possibly know about your case?" he said. "The guy's in jail. All he knows is what he reads in the paper."

"He has the mind of a killer," Avery insisted. "He *thinks* like our guy."

O'Malley frowned.

"Stop," he said, "stop, please. Listen to me, Avery. I like you. I saw you do some amazing things on the beat: fearless, dedicated, honest, and most of all, smart. Other people saw it too. They might give you shit but that's because they're jealous and afraid. People are afraid of what they don't understand, and I'm beginning to feel that fear."

"Captain, what are you—"

A palm stopped her.

"Please," he said, very calm, almost torn, "let me finish. This case, it's a big one. Bigger than I thought. We've got bodies spread out over three counties so far, three dead girls, no further leads, and a lot of pissed off people. You're an animal, Avery. I see it. I see it even now. You're *consumed* by this case. You really want to find this guy, so bad that you've been making some really stupid rookie mistakes."

He held up a finger.

"One," he said, "you harassed a civilian this morning in Cambridge."

"I had reason to believe—"

"I don't care what you believed," he yelled. "You accosted a man in an art shop, a very well-connected man, I might add, a man that's already been through the wringer a hundred times because of his past. Guy had a breakdown after you left. Tried to commit suicide in the bathroom. His boss had to tear down the door. Ambulance was called. Then he called me, and he called the chief, and he called the mayor. And do you know what he said? He said we allowed a psycho to lead this case. Luckily, he hasn't pressed charges, yet."

"Suicide?"

Avery lowered her head. The burning stare of Wilson Kyle came into her mind, and she remembered his passionate speech about Lang's history.

"That was a mistake," she said. "I didn't mean to."

"Two," O'Malley said and held up two fingers. "You got yourself in the papers. Now, I know that's not your fault. You walk around like you're the only person in the universe half the time. Makes me wonder how you can possibly *see* anything, but you do. What you *didn't* see were all these paparazzi scumbags having a feeding frenzy at your expense. The photo from the park I can handle. What I can't handle is that picture from the prison. You went to see the most famous serial killer in Boston's history, a man *you* got off, a man that then killed again in *your* name, and you didn't think to ask? Or watch for cameras? Or to at least give me the heads-up so I could tell you you were nuts?"

"I needed the perspective."

"Then you call me, or Connelly, or anyone else connected to this case. You don't go to a federal prison to hunt down an old flame. I mean, Jesus. Don't you even *read* the papers? They made it look like this entire department is a bunch of morons, and that the only leads we could get had to come from a former flame. It's bad, Avery, real bad."

"Captain, I'm—"

"Three," he said and held up three fingers, "you've got dissention in your ranks. Thompson and Jones are complaining about the surveillance gig."

"They wasted an entire day yesterday!"

O'Malley held up a hand.

"Connelly won't even talk to you—"

"That's not my fault!"

"I don't know what you did to Finley," he said, shocked, "but he's actually been working his ass off and he's genuinely upset about all this."

Suddenly, Avery began to realize where the conversation was headed.

"Upset about all *what*?" she said.

"Maybe I promoted you too soon," O'Malley mumbled to himself.

"Captain, wait."

He shook his head and made a face.

"No more, Avery, please. No more. OK? I've got the chief barking up my ass. The mayor is pissed. I've got complaints coming in from who-the-fuck-knows, and they're all about you. But the worst of it all, seriously," he said with true sorrow in his eyes. "The worst thing is, this isn't about you at all, or any of this petty bullshit. We've got three dead girls in under a week. Three dead, Avery. And no leads. And a dead trail. Am I right?"

Avery flashed on the killer's twirl and bow in the parking lot camera.

"I'm going to find him," she said, "I swear it."

"Not on my watch," O'Malley replied. "You're off the case. Effective immediately. Connelly is taking over."

"Captain—"

"Not a word, Black. Not a word because I'm calm right now, right? I'm calm because this is upsetting to me too, but if you push me I'm going to get really angry because of all the pressure I'm under over this case. You're off. I want all your research on Connelly's desk in the next hour. Any information from the latest crime scene in Belmont. Where are we on that? Where's the body? No, I don't want you to tell me now. I want it all written down, along with any leads you're pursuing, anything. Leave nothing out. Understood? Then you're free to go. Take the rest of the day off. Come back on Monday and we'll talk about what happens next. I need the weekend to think it over."

"I'm off the case," she said.

"You're off."

"For good?"

"For good." He nodded.

"Am I still on homicide?"

O'Malley wouldn't answer.

CHAPTER TWENTY FIVE

Avery had nowhere to go. Her favorite place, the shooting range, was for cops, and she no longer felt like a cop. Her house was dark and empty, and she knew that if she went home, she would simply crawl into bed and remain there for days.

A local pub, right around the corner from her house, was open. She started the morning off right.

"Scotch," she said, "the good stuff."

"We have a lot of good stuff," the bartender replied.

Avery didn't recognize him. She'd only ever visited the bar at night. Not any longer, she thought with reckless abandon. I'm a *day* drinker now.

"Lagavulin!" she demanded and pounded the bar.

There were only a couple of other people in the bar at that hour, all locals, two old men that looked like they drank for a living.

"Another!" Avery called.

After four shots, she was wasted.

Strangely, the sensation reminded her of the past. After Howard Randall had killed again after his release through Avery's genius defense, she'd gone on a bender for weeks. All she remembered from that time were lonely nights in her dark room, and hangovers, and the constant media coverage that seemed to run in a loop.

She stared down at herself, at her hand and clothes and the people in the bar.

Look how far you've fallen, she thought. Not even a cop anymore.

Nothing.

Her father's face came to mind, laughing: "You think you're so special," he'd once told her with a gun pointed at her temple. "You ain't special. I *made* you, and I can *take* you."

Avery stumbled home.

Images of the killer merged with car routes and her father and Howard Randall, and the last thing she remembered before she blacked out was her own sobs.

* * *

Avery spent the rest of the day in bed, the blinds closed. Randomly throughout the afternoon and night, she got up to hydrate or down a beer or stuff her face with leftovers in the refrigerator before she headed back to her room and crashed.

At ten o'clock on Saturday morning, the phone rang.

The caller ID read Rose.

Avery picked up, groggy and still consumed with sleep.

"Hey."

The voice on the other end was tough and unrelenting.

"You sound asleep. Did I wake you?"

"No, no," Avery said and sat up to wipe the spittle from her chin. "I'm up."

"You never answered my email."

"What email?"

"I responded to your email. I said yes to lunch. Are we still on?"

It took a second for Avery to understand what she meant, but then she remembered having emailed Rose at the height of her own excitement, when she thought she was on the verge of catching a killer. Now, hung over, a pariah at work, and not even sure about her own position, she was loath to dress up her misery in clothes and makeup and try to act like a loving mother in front of her estranged daughter.

"Yeah," she said. "Of course. I can't wait to see you."

"Are you sure? You sound terrible."

"I'm just, I'm fine, honey. Noon. Right?"

"See you then."

The line went dead.

Rose, Avery thought with a sigh.

They were strangers. Avery had never admitted it to anyone, but nursing Rose and trying to be a mother had been a nightmare. At the time, the *idea* of motherhood had been beautiful: a new life, the wonder of childbirth, the possibility that Rose could save her relationship with Jack. In *practice*, however, she'd found it to be exhausting, unrewarding, and yet another reason to battle with Jack. Any chance she could get, Avery had hired a nanny, or put Rose in daycare, or handed her over to her ex-husband. Work had been her only refuge.

I was such a bad mother, she thought.

No, she tried to remind herself. It wasn't *all* bad.

She had truly *loved* Rose.

There were plenty of great memories. Sometimes they would laugh and dress up together. Avery even taught her how to wear high-heeled shoes. There were hugs and tears and late-night movies and ice cream.

All of that seemed so far away now.

They'd been apart for years.

After Howard Randall, Jack had filed for custody, and he got it. He said that Avery had been an unfit mother, and cited numerous incidents, including pictures of when Rose had started to cut herself, and texts and emails to her mother that had never been answered.

When was the last time I saw her? Avery wondered.

Christmas, she thought. No, a few months ago. You passed her on the street. You hadn't seen her in so long she was practically unrecognizable.

Now, Avery wanted to be a mother, a *real* mother. She wanted to be the person Rose called for advice and had sleepovers with and went on ice-cream binges.

Pain continued to stand in Avery's way, the endless pain in her heart and stomach over what she'd done in the past, and what she still had to make up for as a detective. It was all consuming, a giant, dark monster that demanded to be fed.

There is no justice.

Avery pulled herself together.

In jeans, T-shirt, and a brown blazer, she stared at herself in the mirror. Too much makeup, she thought. You look tired. Depressed. Hung over.

A bright smile did little to hide her inner turmoil.

"Fuck it," she said.

Jake's Place on Harrison Avenue was a dark, cavernous diner with maroon booths and lots of places where people could enjoy a good meal and remain largely anonymous. On multiple occasions, Avery had spotted movie stars and celebrities. Rose had first picked the location during the custody dispute, and although Avery was sure it was because Rose didn't want to be seen with her own mother, it had become the string that kept them together, and the only place they ever met after long months apart.

Rose was there early, already seated in a booth far away from other customers.

In many ways, she was a clone of Avery when she was young: blue eyes, light brown hair, a model's features, and excellent taste in clothing. She wore a short-sleeved blouse that exposed her toned arms. A tiny diamond nose ring had been placed near her left nostril. With perfect posture and a guarded stare, she gave a perfunctory smile before her features once again turned blank and unreadable.

"Hi," Avery said.

"Hi," was the curt reply.

Avery leaned in for an awkward hug that wasn't returned.

"I like the nose ring," she said.

"I thought you hated nose rings."

"It looks good on you."

"I was surprised by the email," Rose said. "You don't contact me that often."

"That's not true."

"I take that back," Rose thought. "You only contact me when things are going really well, but from what I read in the papers, and from what I can see for myself," she said with a squinted observation, "that's not the case."

"Thanks a lot."

To Avery, who only saw her daughter in spurts every year, Rose appeared far older and more mature than her sixteen years might have indicated. Early admission to college. Full scholarship to Brandeis. She even worked as a nanny for a family near her house.

"How's Dad?" Avery asked.

The waiter came by an interrupted them.

"Hello, there," he said. "My name is Pete. I'm new here so bear with me. Can I get you anything to drink?"

"Just water," Rose said.

"Me, too."

"OK, here are your menus. I'll be back in a minute to take your order."

"Thanks," Avery said.

"Why do you always ask about Dad?" Rose snapped when they were alone.

"Just curious."

"If you're so curious, why don't you call him yourself?"

"Rose—"

"Sorry," she said. "I don't know why I said that. You know what? I don't even know why I'm *here*," she lamented. "To be honest, Mom, I don't know why *you want* me here."

"What's that supposed to mean?"

"I'm seeing a therapist," Rose said.

"Really? That's great."

"She says I have a *lot* of mommy issues."

"Like what?"

"Like, you left us."

"Rose, I never—"

"Hold on," Rose insisted, "please. Let me finish. Then you can talk, OK? You left. You handed custody over to Dad and you were gone. Do you have any idea how that destroyed me?"

"I have *some* idea—"

"No, you don't. I was like, super popular before that whole thing went down. Then, practically overnight, I'm the girl everyone has to stay away from. People teased me. Called me a murderer because my mom let off a killer. And I certainly couldn't talk to *you*, my own mother. I needed you back then. I really did, but you practically abandoned me right then and there. You refused to talk to me, refused to talk about the case. Do you realize that everything I knew about you from that time, I learned from the papers?"

"Rose—"

"And of course, there was no money," Rose laughed with a flip of her hand. "We were broke after you lost your job. You never thought about that, did you? You went from a star attorney to a cop. Great move, Mom."

"I *had* to do that," Avery snapped back.

"We had *nothing*," Rose insisted. "You can't just start a new career over in the middle of your life. We had to move. Did you ever think about that? About how it would *affect* us?"

Avery sat back.

"Is this why you came here? To yell at me?"

"Why did *you* want to come here, Mom?"

"I wanted to reconnect, to see how you were, to talk to try and work things out."

"Well, none of that is going to happen unless we get over *this* first, and I'm not over it. I'm just not."

Rose shook her head and looked to the ceiling.

"You know? For years I thought you were a superstar. Incredible personality, big job, we lived in a great house, and it was like—wow—my mom is amazing. But then it all fell apart, and everything went along with it, the house, the job and *you*—most of all, you."

"My whole life collapsed," Avery said. "I was devastated."

"I was your daughter," Rose complained. "I was there too. You ignored me."

"I'm here now," Avery swore, "I'm here right now."

The waiter came back.

"OK, ladies! Do we know what we want?"

Simultaneously, Avery and Rose yelled: "*Not yet!*"

"Whoa, *OK*. Why don't you just flag me down when you're ready."

No one answered.

The waiter backed away and left.

Rose rubbed her face.

"It's too soon," she realized. "I'm sorry, Mom. But it's too soon. You asked why I wanted to come here? Because I thought I was ready. I'm not."

She edged out of her seat and stood up.

"Rose, please. Sit down. We just got here. I miss you. I want to talk."

"It's not about you, Mom. It was never *just about you*. Don't you get that?"

"Give me another chance," Avery said. "Let's start over."

Rose shook her head.

"I'm not ready yet. I'm sorry. I thought I was, but I'm not."

She walked out.

"Rose! *Rose!?*"

CHAPTER TWENTY SIX

For a long time, Avery remained in the diner booth, alone. She ordered eggs and toast, a small salad, and a cup of coffee and just sat there, going over everything that had been said.

My daughter hates me, she realized.

More depressed than she'd been in years, she wanted to crawl in a hole and die. Instead, she paid the check and walked out.

Sunlight made her cringe.

Why can't it be a *rainy* day? she wondered.

People on the street seemed to race by. Cars whizzed past her view. She stood alone among the activity like a spirit, not yet dead, not truly alive.

This is what the killer wants, she thought. He's in your head. He's laughing at you. Just like Howard. *Just like Howard.*

Avery went back to her car and drove.

Without any conscious thought to a destination, she found herself headed south—toward the prison. The bodies of all three girls kept flashing in her mind, and the killer and the car and the routes and some house, a house she imaged he might live in: small, hidden by trees with an unkempt lawn, because he had better things to do than mow a lawn. Her suspects were discarded, every one of them.

She needed a fresh start. A new perspective.

The prison parking lot was as she remembered. The walk inside was the same. Guards whispered behind her back and pointed. The woman behind the gates chided her for no appointment.

"He said he *knew* you'd back," a guard laughed. "What are you, in love now? I guess I *should* believe everything I read in the papers."

There was no real reason to go back. She didn't actually believe he would help her, or could help her, not after the disastrous turn at Art for Life. He just liked to play games, she understood. But Avery was in the mood for games. She had nothing left to hide, nowhere else to go, and for some strange reason—at that moment in time—Howard Randall seemed like the only *real* friend she had in the world.

Howard sat in the basement meeting room as he had before, only this time, the smile was gone, he appeared concerned.

"You don't look quite yourself today, Avery. Are you all right?"

Avery laughed.

If she had a cigarette, she might have taken it out and begun to smoke. She hadn't smoked since she was a kid, but that's how she felt: reckless, untouchable.

She took seat and placed her elbows on the table.

"Your last tip was bullshit," she said. "An artist? Did you mean John Lang?"

"I don't know who you're talking about."

"*Bullshit!*"

She aggressively smiled.

"You played me," she said. "Nice move. Was that all so we could take a trip down memory lane and you could watch me break down in tears?"

"I take no comfort in your pain," he said in earnest.

"*Fuck you!*" she yelled. "You're playing games with me right now. You told me he was an artist. You practically handed him to me on a platter."

"Your killer *is* an artist," he said. "A *true* artist."

"What's *that* supposed to mean?"

"He takes great pride in his work. He's no random killer. He's no butcher. There is a *purpose* to his cause. These girls *mean* something to him. He knows them, personally, and in exchange for their lives he gives them immortality, in art."

"How can you possibly know that?"

Howard leaned forward.

"You never asked me how I chose *my* victims," he replied, "or *why* they were positioned in such ways."

As Howard's defense attorney, Avery had covered every possible avenue to get him acquitted. One of those avenues had involved understanding the killer's mind and why he had committed such heinous acts, so that she could effectively distance Howard from the murders based on his own personal history.

"It was a statement on people that act dead in real life," she said. "You picked your best students and charged them with some crime against humanity, and then you dismembered them and placed their parts on the ground to look like multiple people trying to escape from the underworld."

"*No*," Howard snapped.

He leaned back.

"What is life?" he urgently asked. "What does it *mean*? Why are we *here*?"

"How is that relevant to anything?"

126

"It's everything!" he yelled and hammered the table.

A guard peeked through the viewing hole.

"Everything all right?"

"Yes, Thomas," Howard said, "I'm just getting, *excited.*"

The guard left.

"Life is short," Howard tried to explain, "and it's cyclical. We live and we die again and again in a constant cycle within this atmosphere. *How* we live—in *this* life—affects all the other times we are reborn, the very energy of ourselves and our world. My victims were chosen because they had flaws, certain flaws that they would never have corrected in *this* life. That's why I had to help them, so they could thrive in the *next* life."

"Is that how you justify your actions?"

"This world is what we make of it, Avery. Anything we wish can be ours. My actions are based on my beliefs. How do you justify *your* actions?"

"I'm trying to make amends for my past, and I do it every day."

He sighed and shook his head and appeared ready to blush, like a man that had finally, startlingly, found the woman of his dreams.

"You're so special," he gushed, "so very special. I knew it the moment I saw you. Tough and smart and funny and yet, flawed, broken by your past. I can help you fix that, Avery. Let me help you. There's still time. Don't you want to be happy, free?"

I want my daughter back, she thought.

"I want to find a killer," she said aloud.

Howard eased forward, as sharp as a hawk.

"How did it feel when your father murdered your mother?"

Avery stiffened.

How does he know about that? she wondered. It was in all the papers, she told herself. It's public record. Anyone can find that information.

"You want to dig up my past again?" she said, "Make me cry? Not today. I'm already at rock bottom. There's nowhere else for me to go."

"Perfect," he said. "Now you can *rise.*"

The day of her mother's death was clear in Avery's mind.

It happened behind the house, after school. She came home and heard the shot. She was only ten at the time. One shot, silence, and then another. A run into the forest and she saw her father there, standing over her body, the shotgun in his hand. "Go get me a shovel," he'd said.

127

"I felt nothing," Avery admitted to Howard. "My mother was a drunk and never there for me. She made it clear I was a mistake. I felt nothing when she died."

"What kind of mother are *you*?"

A crack. Avery felt a crack in the empty, desolate shell of her existence. And although she was empty and depleted, she began to realize she could still be hurt.

"I don't want to talk about Rose."

A deep frown furrowed Howard's brows.

"I see," he said. "I understand."

He searched the ceiling, thought about something else, and turned back to her.

"Your killer knows these girls," he said. "What do they all have in common?"

Avery shook her head.

"The third girl is a mystery for now," she said. "The first two, both in college, both in sororities. One's a senior, one's a junior, so that's no connection."

"No," he whispered.

"What?"

"No," he said again. "You're wrong."

"About *what*?"

Disappointment sank his gaze.

"Have you ever heard the story about the boy and the butterfly?" he asked. "When a caterpillar transforms into a butterfly, the butterfly uses its body and wings to break free from the cocoon. It is a difficult, time-consuming task, but as the butterfly struggles and works, it gains muscle, and strength, and when it finally does breaks free, it is able to launch it into the sky and capture food with ease and *survive*. However, one day, a boy that kept caterpillars as pets saw one of his cocoons shake and move. He felt sorry for the budding creature and wanted to help it, so that it would not have to suffer so much. He asked his mother to cut a slight opening in the cocoon to aid in its escape. But that simple act, born of love and care, robbed the butterfly of its power, and when it finally emerged—all too soon—its body and limbs and wings were not yet strong enough to hunt or fly, and within days, it died."

"What's that supposed to mean?" Avery asked. "Am I the butterfly or the boy?"

Howard wouldn't answer.

128

He simply lowered his head and remained silent, even when Avery continued to ask, and then shout, and then pound on the table for an answer.

CHAPTER TWENTY SEVEN

Agitated.

Avery was agitated by her meeting with Howard, angry and agitated.

What did he *mean*? she wondered. Everything I said was fact. Both in college. Both in sororities. One a senior. One a junior. What was wrong with that?

Arg! she mentally cried.

The streets were filled with people and cars. It was a Saturday, and she was officially off the case. Still, she didn't just want to just kill time. She wanted to *act*. Start from scratch, she thought. The beginning.

Lederman Park was thriving with runners and dogs by the time she arrived. On the baseball diamond near the river was a softball game between men in blue and red.

Avery parked the car and walked to the bench where Cindy Jenkins had been found. The memory of the body was clear in her mind, the placement, the slight smile, and the look toward the cinema. He wanted to kill in threes, she thought. But that changed. Why did it change? Nothing about the three bodies had seemed very different. They were all handled with care, and except for the last body, they were all staring at threes—three women in love, three girls from WWII. What's the connection? she wondered.

She sat down, not on the spot where Cindy had been placed, but on the opposite side of the bench, and searched her phone for any information about the number three: it was a magical number in most religions. It sounds like the word "alive" in Chinese. It was the first number that meant "all." Noah had three sons. The trinity is three. *Three. Three. Three.*

Avery put down her phone.

You wanted to kill three, she thought. There was power in three. But then something changed. What changed? What made you want to kill *more*?

From her meeting with Howard, Avery was beginning to believe the killer had some kind of higher belief system, maybe of a religious god, maybe of his own type of god. A god that needed young girls. Why? Avery thought. Why do you need young girls?

Both in college. Both in sororities. One a senior. One a junior.

No, Howard had said.

She drove to Auburn Cemetery.

130

As she stood before the spot where Tabitha Mitchell had been placed and as she stared across the great cemetery, Avery felt like she was in some kind of surreal world that wasn't completely her own. The drive to Lederman Park. The drive to the cemetery. They were calming, peaceful. *He* would have experienced the same thing. No fears. No worry that he would be caught. Just another beautiful day.

Stony Brook Children's Playground in Belmont was a hotbed of activity. Avery was surprised that the crime scene had already been cleaned up. Children ranging in ages from babies to eight-year-olds could be seen everywhere. The older kids ran through the sprinklers and climbed up and down the wooden castle. Mothers cried out and chased their young. Kids cried from bumps on their heads. Some of the mothers and nannies glared at Avery, as if they knew her or they were trying to place her face.

She headed over to the castle entrance where the third girl had been placed.

A child peeked out from the opening.

"Hi," he said and scrambled away.

Avery imagined the way the girl had looked, and then she turned to stare at the mural with countless children holding hands.

What's the connection? she wondered.

Both in college. Both in sororities. One a senior. One a junior.

No.

She dialed a number.

The gruff voice of Talbot Diggins answered.

"What's up, Black? Thought you were dead."

"Why would I be dead?" she asked.

"Don't you *ever* read the papers? East Coast is in a panic over this killer. Three girls in a week? You're front page news again. Says you're off the case. On official leave."

"I'm not on official leave."

Children could be heard around Talbot. They squealed. He said, "Hold on a sec," and then his voice muffled and she heard, "Quiet, rascals. Can't you see papa's on the phone. Go bother your mother. Get out of here! *Go* I'll be there in a second."

'Sorry," Avery said, "I'm disturbing you."

"Nah," he came back, "just another Saturday in the park. What's up, Black?"

"I called to find out about the third victim."

"Yeah, I got a call from Lieutenant Connelly at your office. He said he's heading up the investigation now. Wanted to know what

131

we found. He sounds like a real dick. Ran her prints through the system and got a match. Was involved in some stupid college prank last year. Her name is Molly Green. Media hasn't been informed yet, so keep this to yourself. She was a Brandeis senior. Finance major. Not a very good student. Not a sorority girl either, so no more 'Sorority Killer.'"

"Did you talk to anyone at Brandeis?"

"Spoke to the dean. Again, very hush, hush for now. He doesn't want anything revealed until he can make his own statement on Monday. He referred me to a guidance counselor named Jessica Givens. Apparently, Molly was having panic attacks about the job market."

"Job market? Did the victim *have* a job?"

"Counselor didn't say. But she *did* tell me that it all worked out in the end."

"Can I have the number for that counselor?"

"Yeah," he said. The phone moved away from his face as he searched for the number and yelled it out so that Avery could hear. "Got that?" Avery typed it into her phone and wrote down the name Jessica Givens. "I got it," she said.

"You talk to her friends?" Avery asked.

"My team reached out to friends and family yesterday. Some are still on it today. She worked as a part-time nanny for a family near the school. Last time anyone saw her alive. Killer snatched her around the house on her way home Thursday night."

"How do you know that?"

"My squad took some testimony from a young kid, fifteen years old, that lives across the street from the house where Molly worked. Kid said he couldn't sleep. At about the time Molly got off from work, he saw a girl that matches her description exit the house and start talking to some guy near a blue minivan."

Avery sucked in a breath.

"That's what he drives," she said, "a blue Chrysler minivan."

"Yeah," Talbot agreed, "that's what your supervisor told me. Said they still had no leads on who owns that car, but they're narrowing down the search. Kid said the perpetrator was wearing a hat and glasses. White guy, about five-six or five-five, lean but strong, between the ages of twenty-five and forty-five. That's your guy, right?"

"That's our guy."

"Kid didn't know what he was seeing. Says it looked like the girl passed out. The guy called for help and then put the girl in the car and drove away."

"Did the kid call anyone?"

"No, he said it looked like the guy was taking care of her. Kid's only fifteen."

"Anything else?"

"That's not enough?"

"Just trying to put all the pieces together."

"You're lucky I'm even talking to you, Black. Shit, that Connelly hates your ass."

"Why are you helping me?"

"I guess I just have a thing for desperate, reckless white chicks that I read about in the papers," he joked, and then his voice muffled again and he said, "Aw, come on, baby. I'm just playing. She's a detective. No, I'm not interested in her. Hold on one sec." Back in the phone he said, "All right, Black, I've got to go. Nice chat."

The line went dead.

Brandeis, Avery thought. The third girl went to Brandeis University in Waltham—the furthest county west so far. The first victim went to Harvard, which is in Cambridge, right next to Boston. The second one went to MIT in Cambridge and was dropped off much further west at the cemetery in Watertown. Brandeis University is even further west, but the victim was taken east, into Belmont.

He lives in either Belmont or Watertown, she realized.

The logic seemed to make sense. He wouldn't have wanted to travel further to find and place each girl he killed. Based on where he dropped off the bodies and took them, his travel time would have been shorter and shorter each time. Lederman is a long drive from out here in Belmont, she thought. All the way to Boston. Still, it was the first body and he wanted to make a statement—*and* create some distance from his home. Then he got bolder. The second body was further west, in Watertown. The third was even further, in Waltham. He can't live in Waltham, she thought. Why would he want to drive all the way to Boston from there?

She called Finley.

Extremely loud and obnoxious heavy metal music could be heard in the background when Finley picked up.

"Yo, yo," he cried.

"Finley, it's Black."

133

In nearly a whisper, she heard, "Oh shit," and then the music went down and Finley was all business. "Look, Black," he said, "I'm not supposed to talk to you about the case."

"Are you still on car dealership duty?"

"Yeah?"

"The killer lives in either Belmont or Watertown. Narrow your search to those two counties and it will save a lot of time."

"How do you know that?"

She hung up.

Accounting. Economics. Finance. All business majors.

Talbot said the third victim was stressed out about job interviews. Cindy had a job lined up at an accounting firm. What was the name? *Devante*, she remembered. Biggest firm in Boston. Did Molly have a job? Tabitha was a junior. Would *she* have a job?

She headed to her car.

On the way to Brandeis, she dialed Finley again.

"*What the fuck!?*" Finley snapped. "Leave me alone. It's Saturday. This is the first time in two years I don't have a shift on a Saturday or Sunday. Let me enjoy myself. Call Connelly. He's on. Call Thompson. He's on too."

"Tabitha Mitchell," she said, "did she have a job lined up somewhere?"

"A *real* job?"

"Yeah, a real job. Not a princess at Disneyland."

"Why would she need a job? She was a junior, right?"

"I don't know. That's why I called you. Didn't you talk to her family?"

"Yeah, the mother."

"She never said anything about a job?"

"No."

"Call her again. Find out if Tabitha had something lined up for the summer."

"I'm off-duty."

"You're in the middle of a case!"

"I don't have to fucking answer to you, Black!"

"*There's a killer on the loose!*" Avery cried, "And he's going to kill again. And I'm close, Finley, real close. I can feel it. Call the mom. Tabitha's friends. Whoever you have to. I need an answer. *Soon.* Please. Call me when you know."

"*Fuck!*" Finley screamed before she hung up.

134

CHAPTER TWENTY EIGHT

Avery took Route 20 all the way to Waltham County. The drive was slow.

Every few miles she had to stop at a light.

Jessica Givens never picked up her phone. After the fourth call, Avery realized it must be her work number. She left a message and called the operator.

"Hi there," she said, "I need the number of a Jessica Givens in Waltham."

"We have *ten* Givenses in Waltham," the operator said. "Do you know where she lives?"

"No."

An answering machine picked up at the dean's office.

Avery drove on South Street directly into Brandeis. It took a while to figure out where to park.

Brandeis was one of the top-ranked financial institutes in the state. The central campus was a series of winding streets on a large hill that was incredibly difficult to navigate and walk. A number of antique-looking brick buildings dotted the property and were occasionally broken up by a stone castle, or a modern glass structure with eccentric architecture. After she parked, she walked up quiet paths and asked anyone she passed where to find the registrar. Eventually, she was directed to a small building that was almost completely empty. A single person worked a counter inside.

"We're closed," he said.

Avery flashed her badge.

"My name is Avery Black. I'm looking for Jessica Givens. I understand she's a guidance counselor that works somewhere on campus."

A very warm, friendly smile greeted her.

"Heyyyy," he said. "You're Avery Black. You hunt serial killers, right? *Cool.*"

"There's nothing cool about a serial killer."

"No, no," he backtracked. "Of course not. I didn't mean the serial killer. I meant *you*. You've been all over the news. I know who you are. They're crucifying you in the papers."

"I'm surprised you're still talking to me."

"Yeah," he smiled, "you're hot."

The words seemed to have slipped out, and when he realized they'd been said aloud, he blanched and blushed and tried to backtrack.

"I'm sorry. That was totally unprofessional. I—"

"It's fine." She flirted with her most winning smile. "*Seriously.*"

"Really?"

"Yeah." She nodded and leaned in close. "Really. Can you help me?"

"Sure, sure. You're lucky I'm still here. I was supposed to be off by now. Let's see," he thought and scanned his computer. "What do you need?"

"The cell phone number and home address of Jessica Givens."

He peeked up over his screen. A lock of his wavy black hair covered one eye. He was young, probably in his early twenties.

"You know, I'm not supposed to give out personal information."

Avery leaned closer.

"What's your name?" she whispered.

"Buck."

"*Buck,*" she said with her lips, and then she lowered her voice and looked both ways as if they were being secretly watched,

"I'm close to finding this killer, Buck. Jessica Givens has information that could help."

Suddenly, he appeared worried.

"Did he attack someone *here*? I thought it was just Harvard and MIT."

"Let's just say no one is safe, Buck. Every college girl is a target. But Jessica Givens," she stressed and pointed toward the door, "she knows something. Something important. A piece of information that could solve this whole case. I can't trust anyone else. I'm on my own here. Can you help me? Just between us. No one else has to know."

"Shit, " he whispered. "Sure," he said. "Sure, if it's that important, *all right*," he cheered, determined, and he gave her what she needed.

"Thank you," she said. "I hope you realize that you could have just single-handedly helped me catch this killer."

"Really?"

"Really," she whispered in her best, seductive voice.

A finger went to her lips.

"Remember, our secret."

136

"*Definitely*," Buck said. "Just between us."

Avery quietly backed away and slipped out the door. The second the sunlight hit her face, she dialed the number given.

"Hello?" someone answered.

"Is this Jessica Givens?"

"Yes. Who is this?"

"Hi, Jessica. My name is Avery Black. I'm one of the investigators on the Molly Green case. I understand you already spoke to Talbot Diggins?"

"How did you get this number?"

"Are you the counselor Detective Diggins spoke with about Molly Green?"

"Yes, I am. But this is a private line. I'm with family right now."

"Molly Green is dead, Ms. Givens. We're trying to track her killer. This will only take a second. You said the victim was stressed about her job interview process, is that right?"

"That's right."

"How was that problem resolved?"

"She received a job offer from an accounting firm about a month ago."

Accounting firm, Avery thought.

Cindy Jenkins was hired by an accounting firm.

"Do you remember the name?"

"Of course," Jessica said, "it's one of the biggest firms in Boston. I was surprised she was hired. Her academic performance wasn't like some of the other students who applied to the same company. It was Devante. Devante Accounting in Boston financial."

CHAPTER TWENTY NINE

Just after sunset on the Bentley University Campus in Waltham, the killer parked his car in a lot to the north of College Drive and walked south, across the pavement.

An uneasy feeling churned in his stomach.

He was on the hunt for his fourth victim, and yet it was such an unexpected activity.

Months before he began to plan for his *first* human kill, he was assured by the voice of the All Spirit—who had guided him in each and every phase of the operation—that *three* was the number of girls needed: three kills to unlock the doors of heaven.

The radical change had come during his drop-off of Molly Green.

As the killer had driven to the predetermined spot for her placement in Belmont, a spot that he was sure would please the All Spirit, an angry voice had screamed in his mind: *More*. It had to be a mistake, he was sure. The All Spirit had only needed three. *More*, the voice had repeated—again and again. Worried, sweaty, and unsure of himself, the killer knew the drop-off for Molly Green would have to be changed to account for the shift. In a panic—and he never panicked—he'd scouted Belmont and was lucky enough to find the children's park with the mural that would at least *hark* to the future and please his god.

He, however, had not been pleased.

A new girl meant not just one, but more, a seemingly never-ending supply.

He had *other* interests, other desires. Animals, for one. His passion for collecting animals off the streets. He loved cats, a wounded bat had even made it into his house once, a creature that he had loved and cared for, before it was given immortality.

Botany was another hobby. No time had been allowed in the previous months to augment his mixtures and test them out on live animal subjects. Everything had been for the All Spirit, a god that had become an increasing presence in his life.

More girls...he thought.

More...

His reward for the trinity was *supposed* to be immortality in human form, and a place in heaven with the other celestial beings. But now, he didn't *feel* immortal, in fact, he felt feverish and extremely emotional. This new game, this new plan, it went against his innermost desires, and he began to think cruel thoughts about the All Spirit.

High in the sky, the face of his god frowned, and a booming echo seemed to shake the land itself: *More!*

Yes, I *know*, the killer mentally shouted to the sky. More! Don't you see, I'm here? I've been watching her? I *know* where she is. The plan is set. The placement is set. Everything is under control! he assured the All Spirit. Only he didn't feel under control.

Unlike the other kills, where he'd been *imperious*, where he had felt the protection of the All Spirit—to the degree that if he'd killed someone in public, in broad daylight, not a single person would have noticed now, all eyes seemed to gaze on him.

Outside of the parking lot was an expansive grass lawn.

A movie screen had been erected.

It was Saturday Night Movie Night at Bentley, and the classic cinema on display was the black and white masterpiece *Casablanca*.

Hundreds of individuals and couples and groups of students were splayed out on the lawn to watch the movie. Some of them were on blankets, others in chairs. The boldest among them had brought wine and beer to the event.

He carried with him a blanket and sunglasses.

His target? A senior named Wanda Voles. A reconnaissance mission the night before had informed him of her destination this night. Apparently on the outs with her boyfriend, she'd decided to come to the movie and be alone. Her friends had begged her not to spend a precious Saturday night at such a lame event, but Wanda had been adamant. "*Casablanca* is like, my favorite movie," she had told those in attendance.

He picked this night for several reasons. One of the main reasons was that in the back of his mind, he hoped she wouldn't show up. The thought had been blasphemous and yet undeniable. "*I don't want to do it! I don't want to do it!*" he'd screamed. The All Spirit had refused to listen. Pain had wracked his body in that moment.

Now, he moved along the outskirts of the large crowd. Every so often, he peeked up to see Humphrey Bogart and Ingrid Bergman embrace or fight.

Wanda sat on the western edge of the lawn, alone but surrounded by other students.

He picked a spot about twenty yards behind her. Wanda's dorm, he knew, was about a ten-minute walk east, through the parking lot and over a number of winding and narrow pathways where they might be alone.

On his blanket, the killer pretended to watch the movie.

Don't do it, his mind blared. Don't do it!

I *have* to do it, he roared back.

The pain in his stomach, like a hand that suddenly closed into a fist, made him curve forward. The All Spirit filled his mind. *More!* the god blared. *More! More! MORE!*

I know, he pleaded. I'm sorry.

No joy could be taken in the movie. Every climactic scene only reminded him of the desperate urgency of his own situation, and the people everywhere, and his guilt. It was wrong, all wrong, and he couldn't say it out loud; he couldn't even think it.

When the credits rolled, Wanda Voles collected her blanket and personal items and headed home. Many of the students remained on the lawn. There was a lot of kissing and laughing. Numerous small exoduses took place along the edges. A few people moved beside Wanda.

He stood up only seconds after Wanda had passed and followed her out. Just another ordinary student, he told himself. *Lies*, his mind blared. Stop it! he fought. *More!* the All Spirit roared. The decree shook him and reverberated throughout his being. To those nearby, he seemed to have an epileptic shiver.

Calm yourself, he thought.

He tracked Wanda through the parking lot. She passed right by the killer's car. A few lines of students were headed in the same direction, only they were further away.

Alone, he thought. She's alone. *Now!*

None of the joy, the ease, and the personal investment were there. The power of the All Spirit had left him. Yet he had to go on. As always, the All Spirit watched and waited.

Wanda was ten feet in front of him. She began to hum a tune.

His ruse was prepared. He would greet her, pretend that he'd come to see the movie with his daughter and then complain about his car tire. She would lower down to help him check the pressure and that's when the needle would be placed. No fuss. No witnesses. Just a young girl that disappeared in a parking lot.

Five feet behind her.

He prepared his needle.

Four feet and she was about to enter a new line of cars.

Three feet and he opened his mouth to speak.

In front of Wanda, a student jumped out from behind a car.

140

"*Rah*!" he roared with his arms up.

Wanda jerked back in fright.

He instantly turned and walked in a perpendicular direction. Behind him, he could hear the boy laughing. "I got you *good*!" Wanda screamed back, "You scared me half to death!" "I'm sorry. I'm sorry," he apologized, "but man, that was *good*! I saw you coming and I just had to do it. What are you up to? It's too early to."

Their conversation faded in the background.

Relief flowed through the killer, a desperate relief at being saved from his crime. It wasn't right, he told himself. I *knew* it wasn't right. I have to rethink. I have to replan. Don't worry. Don't worry, he placated his god. This will be fine. I promise.

High above, the All Spirit growled in disapproval.

CHAPTER THIRTY

A dreamy, surreal quality had taken control of Avery Black.

There was no memory of her final words with Jessica Givens, or when she'd hung up or where she'd put her phone.

She stood in the dark of the Brandeis campus. Ahead of her were a rolling green field and a line of trees and the stars. Behind her were red brick buildings illuminated by lower lights.

Calm down, she told herself.

You've been down this road before.

The memory of her near-assault on John Lang from Art for Life was still fresh in her mind, along with the captain's reprimand and the extended weekend she'd been given to think about her actions.

You were taken off the case, remember?

Not anymore, she answered.

Cindy Jenkins had been hired by Devante. Molly Green had been hired by Devante. What about Tabitha Mitchell?

On the way to her car, Avery dialed Finley. The phone rang numerous times before his voicemail picked up. He's avoiding me, she thought. Five more calls were placed. The results were the same. Every time, Avery left the same message, only with more urgency:

"Finley. We've got a connection. Jenkins and Green were both hired by the same firm in Boston. You have to get back to me. Did Tabitha Mitchell have any kind of job lined up for her senior year? Call me back as soon as you get this."

Avery sat in her BMW and logged onto her dashboard computer.

Devante was a private company based in Boston.

General information was all she could find online: the founder of the company, chairman of the board, the CEO, and the statewide structure.

A quick search revealed the vast number of jobs within an actual accounting firm: staff accountant, junior and senior level accountants, tax manager, tax auditor, CPA…. The list was seemingly endless.

Who hires college girls? she wondered. It has to be some kind of human resources head that scouts out colleges and finds likely applicants. That person would most likely then take resumes and distribute the promising ones to the people in charge of whatever positions happened to be open within the company.

How would I find out who scouted and saw the resumes of those two girls?

The answer was obvious, and tricky given her currently diminished status within the Homicide division. You have to get to the Chairman or the CEO, she realized. Only they can give you access to the right people. She laughed. OK, how do I do *that*? A warrant, she thought.

You're going to need a warrant.

Warrants were difficult to get. Probable cause was necessary. In this case, Avery was confident that the connection between the girls and the company that planned to hire them was enough probable cause for a warrant. However, a judge would also want to know that items connected to the crime might be found at the offices of Devante. That might be a problem, she thought, unless the affidavit included computer information. If the killer has anything related to the case on his computer, I can use that to bolster a warrant.

Sleep on it tonight, she thought. Don't make a mistake. Wait for Finley to call. Get everything in place before you go to the captain.

Her mind blared back: *Not on your life.*

She put the car in gear and headed out.

CHAPTER THIRTY ONE

Avery sauntered into the A1 police department at just past ten in the evening. The first-floor receptionist was dealing with an officer and a prostitute. Throughout the rest of the office, plainclothes officers booked drunken college students and took statements. A fight broke out in the back and it took three cops to subdue a tremendous white man.

Police jobs weren't like normal jobs.

The majority of officers didn't just come in at eight or nine and leave at five everyday. Similarly, weekends were almost *never* free unless an employee had seniority or the entire department was on a revolving schedule. In the A1, everyone worked in shifts—five-day shifts that could be from Wednesday to Sunday, and if someone was on a case, they could work all night, every night, and well into the morning.

Avery recognized a few familiar faces. However, no one seemed to pay her much mind. Weekend night shifts had a certain feel to them, like being in a cemetery after staying up for forty-eight hours straight: everyone was in a haze and had a rhythm all their own.

On the second floor, Connelly was arguing with Thompson.

Thompson looked like two men rolled into one, a giant that loved to hit the gym, and combined with his pale skin and full lips and light blond hair, he usually made other police—and perpetrators—extremely uncomfortable.

"Why am I still here?" Thompson complained.

"Are you fucking kidding me?" Connelly snapped. "I just gave you a job and you didn't do it. I don't care if you're here until *four* AM."

"Car dealerships!?" Thompson roared and stood to his full height. "How many fucking dealerships are open on Saturday night? My shift ended hours ago. Here's a list from Watertown and Belmont."

"I asked for Waltham, too. And I asked you for numbers, and for the direct contacts at each company. I don't see anything here for Belmont," he complained and flipped through a list.

Avery sat back on someone's desk and waited for them to finish.

Connelly glanced up.

"What the fuck are you doing here? Didn't the captain tell you to take a rest?"

"Can we talk?" she asked.

"No," he said. "I've got nothing to say to you. Get lost. You're not back until Monday."

She indicated Thompson.

"You're wasting his time."

"I told you!" Thompson followed. "This is a waste of my fucking time."

"*Shut the fuck up!*" Connelly snapped and pointed in his face. "Black, I swear to God. If you're not out of my sight in five seconds I'm going to personally see you off Homicide and back to beat for the rest of your life."

Avery lowered her head.

"I'm not going anywhere," she said in a calm, even tone. "And you need to listen to me. I've got a lead. A big one," she emphasized and looked him right in the eyes. "We need to talk this through. And we need to be on the same team. Do you want to catch a killer? Or do you want to stay pissed off at me because you *think* you know me, or because I was assigned to your team, or because I used to have a better life than you?"

She pushed off the desk.

"I'm sorry if I've done anything to offend you," she said, "but I'm right here. Right now. Just like you. Swimming in the shit. And I haven't let up on finding this killer, and I've finally got a lead. This can't wait until Monday. If you kick me out, I'll just call the captain, and then the chief, and then anyone else who will listen to me."

Thompson pointed at Avery with heartfelt concern.

"Listen to her," he pleaded.

"*Shut the fuck up, Thompson! Sit down.*"

He curled a finger at Avery and pointed to the conference room.

"Three minutes," he said. "You've got three minutes."

Once they were alone, Avery laid it out. "I know I've made some mistakes."

"*Some!?*"

"*Stupid* mistakes," she added, "but it was all in the line of duty. I made a few other mistakes today. I went back to see Howard Randall."

Connelly howled and waved a hand.

"*He gave me a clue*," Avery continued, "or," she added, "something like a clue. I couldn't figure it out until I went to Brandeis."

Connelly slapped his head.

"You went to Molly Green's college? You were told to stay *off* this case."

"*Will you shut up!*" she yelled. "Just for once? Please?"

Surprised, he folded his arms and stood back.

"I talked to someone in the guidance department. She told me that Molly had a job lined up with Devante Accounting. Well, guess what? Cindy Jenkins also had a job with Devante. I don't know about Tabitha yet. Finley was supposed to talk to the mother. I haven't heard back from him. Tabitha was a junior, but if she was hired by them too, that's too much of a coincidence to ignore, don't you think?"

"Your last connection turned out to be shit."

"But it was a *connection*, the only one between two of those girls, until now. If we can link the third girl to Devante, we'll be closer than we've ever been."

"Finley's off duty," he mumbled.

"So?"

Connelly walked away and mulled over the situation. In a gray suit and blue shirt that appeared too small for his muscular frame, he rolled his shoulders and rubbed the blondish stubble on his skin, seemingly annoyed but intrigued.

"Wait here," he said.

"What are you—"

"*I said wait!*" he snapped and walked out.

Beyond the glass, she could see him give instructions to a very flustered Thompson before he went to his own desk and started to make a call.

Avery sat in the conference room for nearly twenty minutes. With nothing to do, the burden of her knowledge finally out, she felt more relaxed and oddly comforted. An intense desire to call her daughter made her reach for the phone.

What would you say? she wondered.

Tell her that you were an idiot, and that you still are. Tell her the truth: that you love her and you'll make this right, no matter what.

The conference door opened.

"Tabitha Mitchell was a junior," Connelly said. "She was graduating early, top of her class. And she was offered a job at Devante Accounting."

Avery sat up.

"Holy shit."

The connection was there. Howard Randall had been right. His words rang out: *He has to find them, watch them, know them from* somewhere. When she went down the list with Randall—one a senior, one a junior—he'd said *no.*

He knew, she realized.

The sickness Avery had felt at having to visit Randall and ask for help now began to wash away. The connection had been made, and if she could fit all the pieces together, there was hope: for her, for her future, to leave the past behind.

"Three of them," Connelly said. "*All* of them had jobs at Devante."

"How did you find out?"

"Finley's been calling the Mitchell house. I called the mother's cell. She was sleeping. Started crying the second I told her it was about her daughter. But she had the information we needed. What's fucked up is, I think the papers said the same thing yesterday or the day before."

That's how he knew, Avery realized. Randall read the papers.

They both stared at each other in silence.

"What do we do now?" she asked.

"You tell me."

She glanced away and bit down on her lower lip.

"We need a name. Who was the hiring manager that met with all those girls?"

"Whoever it is," Connelly said, "he must know that at least two of the girls he hired are dead. It's been all over the news."

"If two girls *you* hired were found dead in under a week, would *you* call someone?"

"Not if I was guilty."

Connelly immediately put the conference room phone on speaker and called the captain. Agitated and sleepy, a remote O'Malley listened to both Avery and Connelly on speakerphone and took his time before he answered.

"Wait until the morning," he said. "There's nothing we can do right now. I'll call the chief and the mayor first thing Sunday. Shit," he mumbled. "Devante. They're huge."

147

"We'll start with the CEO and work our way down," Avery said. "Someone has to have a list of names and job titles. I'm assuming our killer works in human resources."

"Try to get some sleep tonight," the captain said, "both of you. It might be a big day tomorrow. I'll meet you in the office at eight. Avery, if you can't sleep, start on the warrants: one for the company and one for an unnamed individual within the company. You can also call Devante and see if there's a weekend staff. I doubt anyone will pick up at this hour, but it's April. You never know."

The line went dead.

Uneasy in his stance, Connelly refused to look at her.

"Let's hope this works out," he said and left.

Avery completed as much paperwork as she could on two warrants. She called at least ten numbers listed for Devante's Boston office. No one answered.

Go home, she told herself.

Sleep was the furthest thing from her mind.

CHAPTER THIRTY TWO

Sunday felt like a Monday for Avery.

She was up and energized at seven. Strangely enough, she slept like a baby the moment she'd arrived home, probably the best night's sleep she'd had in months.

She threw on a black pantsuit and white button-down. As always, she wore black Skechers sneakers on her feet. The days of high-heel Manolo Blahniks were long gone. After breakfast and a cup of coffee, she stood in her foyer and stared at herself.

Go get him, she said.

A twinge of doubt invaded her thoughts. There had been so many close calls already, so many leads that had turned up dead. No, she thought. This is the one. It *has* to be.

On the way to her car, she surveyed the landscape of her life as a cop: traffic duty, petty crimes, domestic disputes, gang warfare, and now this, her biggest case, a homicide detective on the trail of a serial killer. This is what you've been working toward for the last three years, she told herself: a chance to make amends for the past, to close the Howard Randall chapter for good and to step out of the shadows of miserable regret, and live.

Weekend morning shifts at the A1 changed at eight. Most of the office was empty from the transition, with a large majority of the force either on the streets or on their way into work. Connelly was already there, along with the chief and Thompson.

The chief was in jeans and a red BPD T-shirt, the most casual Avery had ever seen him. On the phone, he waved her into his office with the rest of the group.

"Hold on," O'Malley said into the line, "I've got Black here. Let me put you on speaker and we can get this handled right now."

A gravelly voice emanated through the room.

"Hello? Can everyone hear me?"

O'Malley mouthed "The mayor."

"We're here," he said.

"Detective Black," the mayor said as if the words were distasteful in his mouth, "I hear you've been relentless on this case, even after you were dismissed. How sure are you about Devante? You know Miles Standish is a good friend of mine."

O'Malley mouthed "The owner."

"I highly doubt that Mr. Standish has anything to do with this," Avery said. "We believe the killer is someone within his offices, most likely a human resources manager or liaison that would have met with these girls, read their resumes, and then passed them on to the proper departments."

"I asked how *sure* you are about Devante, Ms. Black. Are you *positive* this is the best lead? I have a very difficult call to make."

"Three girls are dead," she said. "Each one of them is from different schools, and yet they all had jobs lined up at Devante. It's the only connection that makes sense. I'm one hundred percent sure."

"Good," the mayor said. "Mike," he added, "I'll call Miles now. Expect to hear from him soon. If he doesn't cooperate, get your warrant and do what you have to do. I want this case wrapped up by Monday."

"Yes sir," O'Malley said.

When the mayor hung-up, O'Malley addressed the group.

"OK," he said, "here's how we'll do this. Avery, you're lead. That shit you pulled the other day was way out of line, but since you cracked this thing, you should see it through. We'll discuss your future later on. Connelly is your supervisor. You'll have Thompson and whomever else we can pull together once we have all the information. Thompson." he said and paused for a minute to find the right words, "I used to think you were this freakish Irish giant that would come into this office and make things happen. Sadly, none of that happened In fact, I think you're lazier than Finley. Scratch that," he instantly corrected, "I was wrong about Finley. He's been working his ass off. Everyone makes mistakes. You, however, had better amaze me today. Is that understood?"

"Yes, sir," Thompson swore.

Fifteen minutes later, the call they'd been waiting for arrived. O'Malley instantly touched speakerphone.

"O'Malley here," he said.

A perky young voice filled the room.

"Hi there!" she said. "This is Laura Hunt. I'm the personal assistant to Mr. Miles Standish. I was told to call and provide whatever information you might need about Devante."

O'Malley waved at Black.

"You're on," he said.

"This is Avery Black," she said. "I'm not sure if you've been informed, but we have a serial killer on the loose with a possible connection to the Devante Accounting Firm."

"Yes, Ms. Black, I've been fully briefed."

150

"What we need is a name, someone that would have met with each of these college students and then either offered them jobs, or rerouted them to another department within the company where they were hired."

"OK," she said. "Can I ask which Devante firm we're talking about?"

"What do you mean?"

"Well, we have offices in Boston, Chicago, and San Antonio."

"The Boston office."

"OK, hold on one second. Here it is. Timothy McGonagle is the president of Human Resources for the Boston office. I don't think he deals directly with college recruiting, but you can either talk to him or someone on his staff," and she offered his cell phone number, home number, and home address.

"How many people does McGonagle have under him?" Avery asked.

"There are twenty-eight other human resources workers."

"If I have problems, can I call you directly?"

"Absolutely," she said and gave Avery her number. "Mr. Standish wants to help in any way possible. He simply asks that you try and keep the Devante name out of the papers if possible. We wouldn't want people to associate any crimes with our accounting firm."

"Understood," Avery said.

The phone call ended shortly after and O'Malley surveyed the group.

Avery wanted to see Timothy McGonagle for herself, up close and personal. Even if he wasn't the person directly responsible for the crimes, it was becoming almost certain that he hired a killer, or he hired someone that had hired a killer. A quick background check revealed nothing on McGonagle: not even a parking ticket.

"All right," he said, "get to it. I have a sweet sixteen to attend."

* * *

McGonagle wasn't far from the A1. He lived in the affluent neighborhood of Beacon Hill just north of the offices, close to Lederman Park. Connelly stayed behind to oversee two gang-related squads and to try and pull together a team for Avery if needed.

Thompson was assigned as her partner for the day. He kept his mouth shut for most of the ride and sat awkwardly in Avery's passenger seat, his body scrunched in tight.

"Where you from?" Avery casually asked.

"Boston," he mumbled.

"Where in Boston?"

"All over."

"What made you want to be a cop?"

A frown appeared on his albino-like face, and his fat lips curled in a sneer.

"What is this? Twenty questions?" he barked.

Avery parked on Pinckney Street.

McGonagle lived in a large, brick-faced home with white shutters and a red door sunken into an outdoor foyer space. Thompson remained on the edge of the entrance and looked like he wanted to be anywhere but around Avery Black. His size and strange appearance, however, were a magnet for people that walked by; even if they were on the other side of the street, they crossed and stared closely into his face as they passed.

The bell rang and was quickly answered.

"Hello?" someone called.

Tim McGonagle was younger than Avery had expected, maybe in his mid-thirties, with black hair and bright green eyes that seemed to always be calculating figures. He was dressed in gray slacks and a pink button-down shirt and a green tie.

Five eight or five nine, she thought. Too tall. The height doesn't match up.

"Can I help you with something?" he asked.

"Avery Black," she said, "Boston Homicide."

"Yes, I see. A celebrity officer in person." He smiled.

He noticed Thompson before he turned back to Avery.

"What can I do for you?"

"Have you been following the serial killer case?" Avery asked.

"I have," he said.

"Are you aware that three of the victims were recently hired by your firm?"

"No," he said, "my god, that's awful."

'What exactly do you do at Devante?"

He waved inside.

"Would you like to sit down?"

"No, thank you."

A female voice called out from somewhere deep in the home.

152

"Timmy? Who is it?"

"Hold on one second, Peg," he called. "I'm the president of the Devante Human Resources Department for the Boston Division," he said to Avery. "My main responsibilities are to hire and manage the staff. I oversee problems within the company, any major employee/employer disputes, things of that nature. The only resumes I see are for high-level staff we may need, such as a CEO position or a head auditor."

"Who recruits for the colleges?"

"One of my employees. His name is Gentry Villasco, but honestly, I can't imagine him doing anything like this. He's an administrative director. He heads up a team of four. They oversee colleges, college resumes, and they do scouting on campuses."

"If a college student wanted a position at your firm, they'd have to go through him?"

"That's right. His team might sift through applicants and weed out the best resumes, but eventually they'd go to him. If Gentry liked what he saw, he would then pass them onto the appropriate department where a position had opened."

"Can you tell me anything about him? Is he single? Married? What does he like to do on weekends? Does he have friends?"

Timothy laughed.

"Gentry is definitely not a killer," he said. "He's a loner, that's for sure, a little older than I am. Maybe in his fifties? Has a house out in West Somerville. Commutes to work. He's a people-person but he keeps to himself, if you know what I mean? He's worked at Devante longer than I have, about fifteen years."

Avery gave him the hard stare.

"Are you sure you have no knowledge of the three victims in question? Let me tell you their names again, in case you forgot: Cindy Jenkins, Tabitha Mitchell, and the last one hasn't hit the papers yet. Molly Green."

"I've never heard of any of them," he said and then instantly corrected himself. "Well, I've heard of the first two, but not within the company. I read the papers. I'm familiar with the case," and he stood taller and held her gaze.

"Are you going to be home all day?" Avery asked.

"Well, my family and I are planning on going to church in a little while. We're just having breakfast with the kids."

He seemed both honest and genuinely disturbed by the connection to Devante. A family man, Avery thought. She stepped back and tried to imagine a killer with a wife and family.

153

"Here's my card," she said. "Please call me if you can think of anything else."

"Of course," he said. "I'm sorry to hear about all this."

Thompson was leaning on the brick facade with his foot kicked up, oblivious to everything except the sky.

Avery slapped him in the chest as she walked past.

"*Hey!*" he complained.

"Next time you want to act like a doorstop," she said, "go back to the office."

CHAPTER THIRTY THREE

A quick conversation with Laura Hunt and Avery was in possession of the cell phone number and address of Gentry Villasco, as well as the names, addresses, and contact information for everyone on his team, just in case Villasco turned out to be a dead end.

Of the four people who worked for Gentry, two were women and two were men. The women lived in Chelsea and Boston, respectively, both well outside of Avery's general range of the killer's home. The first man commuted from South Boston, also outside the range. The last one lived in Watertown: Edwin Pesh. Watertown was one of Avery's hotspots. She circled his name and hopped in the car. As she drove, Thompson plugged in all the names into the database for a background check. One of the girls had ten outstanding parking tickets. The man from South Boston had been arrested for drunk and disorderly conduct a year earlier. No records were found on the other two.

Gentry Villasco lived on a wide-open street in Somerville. His house was a very small, narrow, two-level Tudor home painted white with brown trim and a brown roof. Multiple trees shaded his driveway. A white Honda Civic was parked before a closed garage.

Avery and Thompson were in the middle of a heated debate.

"I'm just saying, *try* to look like you care," Avery sighed.

"I *do* care," he said.

"Look around," she said. "If I'm talking to a suspect, observe the premises, put on a smile, pretend to take notes. Whatever. Don't just stare at the sky."

"I've been a cop a lot longer than you have."

"Really? That's hard to believe. When was the last time you were promoted?"

Thompson pinched his lips in anger and tried to reposition himself in the tiny space of the BMW passenger seat.

When they exited the car and walked up to the front door, Avery was slightly ahead, with the hulking Thompson behind her like a bodyguard ready to devour any opposition.

The doorbell rang.

A gracious, humble man appeared to greet them. He reminded Avery of a monk, or of some saintly being. Tan and balding on the top with cropped white hair on the sides, he had eyes that were small and squinted. Everything about him was small—his chin, his

155

hands and shoulders. He wore tan slacks and a black sweater over a T-shirt, even though it was at least eighty-five degrees outside.

He's the right build, Avery thought. A little small, but if he was wearing a disguise, he could have also been he wearing heights.

"Hello," Villasco said in the sweetest, most gentle voice imaginable. "Would you like to come in?"

Surprised, Avery said, "Do you know why we're here?"

"Yes,' he nodded with a sad frown, "I think I do."

He turned and headed back inside

"Mr. Villasco, where are you going?" Avery called. "Mr. Villasco, can you please just—excuse me, sir? I need to see."

She and Thompson shared a look.

'Call it in," she said and pulled her gun.

Thompson drew his own gun.

"I'm with *you*."

"Not a chance," she snorted and pointed to the lawn. "You call it in. Wait for the others. I work better on my own."

The house was extremely cold, possibly through central heating as Avery hadn't noticed any air conditioners. She closed the door behind her and stepped inside.

Beyond the gray-blue foyer was a staircase to a second level. A gray cat with green eyes watched her from one of the steps. She turned right and into a small living room. Lots of plants lined the windowsills and hung from the ceiling.

Her heart was racing fast.

The gun was held low.

"Mr. Villasco?" she called. "Where are you?"

"In my office," he replied.

Slowly, she headed toward a small doorway at the back of the living room. After every step, she turned to make sure she wasn't followed. Only once in her life had she been shot. She took two bullets: one in the leg and one in the shoulder.

Gentry Villasco sat behind a large mahogany desk on the right. A green lamp was on one side of the desk, and paperwork was stacked on the other. His hands were hidden in his lap. A small green couch was on Avery's left, under a window.

"Mr. Villasco," she said, "please show me your hands."

"You work so *hard*," he sighed, "all your life."

"Mr. Villasco. I really need to see those hands."

"It's all for *family*. You know that, right? I did it for family."

"Please—your hands."

156

"It just seems *right*." He nodded. "I've already lived. What do I need to be here for anyway? My wife died of cancer two years ago. Did you know that? Terrible disease."

Avery inched closer toward the desk.

"Your hands!"

"Those girls," he said. "I knew, I knew. A horrible tragedy. It truly is. But who are we to judge? Everyone deserves to exist."

He quickly lifted a gun from his lap and placed it under his chin. The weapon had to be at least fifty years old, a six-shooter: silver with a white handle, like something that could be bought at a garage sale, or from an antique shop.

Avery raised a hand.

"Don't do it," she cried.

Villasco fired.

CHAPTER THIRTY FOUR

"*No!*"

The shot echoed through the room. His head jerked from the blast and blood shot out from the back and sprayed the wall behind him.

"Shit," Avery whispered.

Thompson ran in with his gun aimed at everything.

"*What the fuck?!*" he cried. "Oh shit."

Avery turned to him.

"Did you call it in?"

"Everyone's on the way."

Avery stood there staring at the dead man, just a few feet before her, who had been alive but moments before, and her heart broke in a million pieces.

* * *

Gloves and bags were retrieved from her car. Thompson was given a set and told to check the perimeter. Avery took the first floor.

In the living room, carpets were gray and walls were painted a muddy white. Apart from the living room and Villasco's office, there was a kitchen on the opposite side of the stairs. Kitchen cabinets were dark wood. The counters were dark blue and the floors white tile.

A small door led to a grassy backyard enclosed by a wooden fence. All different kinds of flowers were in bloom along the fence, and there as a dark gray patio setting for guests.

Back in the house, Avery found a door to the basement behind the steps. Creaky wooden stairs led to a wholly ordinary space: cement floor, nice wooden shelving along the walls, and other storage areas. She opened a plastic container and found clothing for the winter.

On the first level, she bumped into Thompson.

"Nothing outside," he said. "Garage is filled with cans and gardening tools."

Together, they headed to the second floor.

Avery took the lead, gun held low. The cat she'd seen earlier scurried across the top steps and disappeared. She put two fingers to her eyes and pointed them left. Thompson nodded, turned left at the stairs, and moved down the hallway. Avery went into the cat room. The small guest bedroom was painted a grayish green. Three cat litter boxes rested on wooden floors. Two cats were on the bed, the fat, gray one she'd seen before, and a white kitten. The only closet held moth-ridden, female clothing.

She moved around the banister in the direction where Thompson had headed. The master bedroom to her right held a large bed. Multiple mirrors lined the walls. The carpet was white. She opened a few of the mirrored doors to find clothing and shoes.

"Hey, Black," she heard, "up here."

The last room was more like a closet with a short staircase up to an attic. The space was too small for Thompson to fit inside. Instead, he sat on the steps and pulled down an item from above for Avery to investigate.

"Two others up here as well," he said.

Avery grabbed a furry statue.

It was a cat, a black cat that had been stuffed and mounted on a wooden base. No inscription lined the wood.

"Is there a tabby up there, too?" she asked.

"How did you know?"

Thompson handed down another taxidermy statue. It was a smaller, orange-colored cat with black lines and dark eyes. She handed it back.

"Bag some of those hairs," she said.

"Just this one?"

"Yeah. Forensics found tabby hairs on the first two bodies."

Police sirens could be heard in the distance. As they moved closer, Avery headed downstairs and walked out the front door.

She should have been ecstatic, or relieved.

Instead, Avery felt empty, unsettled. Puzzle pieces swirled in her mind, unconnected: the killer's car routes had all headed north and west outside of Boston. *He* lives northwest of Boston, she thought. It's a match. That didn't explain the blue minivan heading even further west outside of Cambridge. A second house, she thought. He must have a second house. That's where he keeps the minivan. Everything else fit. He grew flowers. Cats lived in the house.

If the tabby cat hairs matched what Randy had found on the bodies, and if some of those plants were psychedelic, Avery knew the case would be closed.

Thompson appeared behind her.

She glanced over her shoulder.

159

"See what you can find in the office," she said. "Try not to disturb the body. We need a second house. And we need to find that dark blue minivan. You're looking for rent bills, a mortgage address, auto insurance forms, anything like that."

"On it."

The last words of Villasco were seared into her mind.

I did it for family.

Who are we to judge?

Everyone deserves to exist.

* * *

Avery watched as Somerville and Boston PD cruisers raced down the street with sirens blaring, parked wherever they wanted, and exited their vehicles with guns drawn.

Connelly was among them.

None of the anger he routinely harbored against Avery was visible in his gaze, none of the uncertainty or distrust. Wonder appeared on his face, a sense of disbelief that what he witnessed could possibly be true: that a woman—a disgraced public figure turned cop—had done it again, solved another case and made the rest of the force look like slugs.

"What have we got?" he said.

Somerville police began to surround the house and enter.

The entire scene unfolded like a dream. Avery could barely see Connelly or the others. She was miles away in her own mind. The puzzle wasn't complete, and yet she had no real facts to base it on except for instinct and Gentry Villasco's last words. *I did it for family. Who are we to judge? Everyone deserves to exist.*

Could Gentry have abducted all those women? Avery wondered. He seemed sweet, almost hapless, like he was roped into something he couldn't control.

"Avery. Are you all right? Talk to me," Connelly insisted.

"He's inside," she said, "Gentry Villasco. Dead. Shot himself. Said something about doing it for family. Thompson is looking for a paper trail that might lead to the minivan or another home."

"Is this our guy? Avery?"

Everyone deserves to exist.

"I have to make a call," she said.

Avery walked out into the street and dialed Tim McGonagle. His phone went directly to voicemail. She left a message.

160

"Mr. McGonagle," she said, "this is Avery Black. I need to know if Gentry Villasco has any family that might work with you in the office, a cousin or nephew—anyone. This is extremely important. Please call me back as soon as you can."

The list she'd taken earlier, of all the people that worked under Villasco, was unfolded and scanned. A circle surrounded the name Edwin Pesh.

You can't just leave a crime scene, she told herself. This is *your* crime scene. Connelly would never forgive you. *O'Malley* would never forgive you. You have to follow through. Take statements, complete a more thorough search of the house.

Patience had never been one of Avery's strong suits. Although her outwardly calm and sarcastic demeanor had—over the years—lulled a lot of people into a false sense of security, inside she was really a machine that refused to stop.

If Villasco is your killer, he's dead now, she reasoned. There's nothing more you can do. The house is being watched and searched.

You can't leave, she mentally cried.

Avery turned back to the house. There was no sign of Thompson or Connelly. A few of the Somerville police talked amongst themselves. Children had begun to creep up to the scene from further down the street, as well as parents in nearby homes.

Go, she thought and made a beeline to her car.

No one stopped her.

The Watertown address of Edwin Pesh was thirty minutes away from the Somerville house of Villasco. Just a short trip, she told herself. If you don't see anything unusual, you turn around and come back. Say you went for a coffee run, or you were sick.

Avery took her time. She slowed down at stop signs and kept her speed under the limit. There's no need to rush, she thought.

About halfway into her ride, she imagined Rose, distressed from their lunch and in a miserable mood all weekend long.

You have to make things right with her, she mulled. No matter what happens here she's your daughter, and not that crying, pooping, and peeing lump anymore. She's a woman now, a real person, and she needs a mother.

She dialed her number.

Voicemail picked up.

"OK, I'm an idiot," Avery said. "Rose, this is your mom. God, I don't even deserve to call myself that, do I? I know I haven't been there for you. I've probably never been there for you the way you needed. I was a terrible mother. That's true, I know it. But I was

161

young, and stupid, and having a child is *hard*. That's not an excuse," she immediately corrected. "This is all on me. Jack was great, he really was great, especially with you. Give me another chance, Rose. I hate what's happened to us. Please. One more chance. I promise to make amends for the past. You might not accept me as a mother anymore, but I'd like to at least try to be."

Voicemail cut her off.

"Shit," Avery whispered.

She was about to call back when she entered Watertown. The area wasn't as familiar to her as Cambridge or Boston. At a stoplight, she plugged in the address for Edwin Pesh and watched the red dot blip on her screen.

Five minutes away.

Two.

The house of Edwin Pesh was in a dismal state. Grey paint was chipped off the wood-panel exterior. A blue shutter hung from a single latch, and the roof was piled with leaves and branches. Unlike any other house on the block, trees enveloped the entire property in a gloomy shade. The lawn hadn't been cut in months, and any flowers were limp or dead.

A dark blue minivan sat in the driveway.

This is it, she thought. This is his house.

Everything came back to her: her conversations with Randall, the car routes from Lederman Park and Cambridge, the abduction of Cindy Jenkins, and the killer, as he bowed and twirled and entered his vehicle to drive away.

She kept the car at a slow roll and moved right up the street. At the intersection, she turned and parked. An extra clip was shoved in her back pocket. A powerful, portable flashlight was attached to her belt. The walkie-talkie was left in the car seat.

Don't go in there alone, she thought. Call for backup.

What if he has another victim? she wondered. Right now, you have the element of surprise. Don't make a scene. Go in alone. Silent. Quick.

You need help! she fought.

For a second, she thought about calling Connelly or Thompson, or even Finley. No, she argued, not them. *Why?* she demanded. You don't trust Connelly or Thompson, and Finley is a loose cannon.

A voice came into her head, one of the speakers at her police academy graduation, a woman who had said, "Everyone needs help. You're not alone as a police officer. You're part of a team. Rely on them."

162

For years, she'd been on her own. No one had been her friend after her world had collapsed. During her early years on the force, nearly everyone had been an enemy. Strangely, one person stood out in recent memory: Ramirez. From the start, he'd been honest with her, and appreciative, and a true partner in every sense of the word. He's hurt, she thought. Out of commission. Still.

She dialed his number.

Ramirez picked up on the first ring.

"Where you been, Black?" he said. "Heard O'Malley took you off the case. What the hell happened?"

"Where are you?" she said.

"I'm at home. Hospital let me go. I'm not supposed to do any strenuous lifting for a while but I'm bored *out of my mind*. Please tell me you're in my hood."

"I found the killer," she said. "His name is Edwin Pesh. He lives in Watertown. I'm right outside his house."

"Whoa."

"How soon can you get here?"

"Did you call it in?"

"I called *you*," she said.

"All right," he muttered and thought it through. "All right."

"Take down this address," she said and gave him the details.

"I'll be there in twenty minutes," he replied, "maybe sooner if I blow all the lights. Don't go in there without me, understand?"

She hung up.

As if she were just another stroller on a balmy Sunday afternoon, Avery shut her car door and headed down the street.

Her heart was beating fast.

At the house, she crouched low and ran up the drive.

She placed a hand on the back of the minivan and stared at the side of the house. No lights were on. The interior was slightly visible through the first and second floor windows. Basement windows had been painted black.

Her fingers ran over the license plate and instantly felt an extremely sticky substance around the edges. Minivan, she thought. Fake license, taped on. *Family*. Villasco had talked about. The dark house loomed above. In one of the windows, she spotted a gray cat.

Probable cause.

Avery drew her gun.

163

CHAPTER THIRTY FIVE

Edwin Pesh was having a tormented weekend. The All Spirit refused to leave him alone. No sleep had come on Saturday night; the voice in his head had continually asked for *more, more*, and the many responsibilities he *still* had to deal with on his own began to take a toll.

Beaten down and weary, he sat in one of the rooms on his second floor surrounded by cats. Cats of all shapes and varieties purred and tried to sit in his lap. There were at least ten of them in that room alone. Some stared out the windows. Others slept in corners or on the single bed, or they ate from one of the many food dishes available on the wooden floors.

Wanda Voles...the name of Wanda Voles was repeatedly mentioned by the All Spirit, so much so that Edwin knew what he had to do. Pick yourself up, he thought. Take care of the cats, walk the dogs, and then go back to Bentley *and get Wanda Voles.*

No! his mind screamed.

Yes! he screamed back.

A bark came from downstairs, and then multiple barks.

Instantly alert, Edwin stood up and looked out the windows.

The backyard was empty.

On the side of the house, someone was crouched behind his minivan.

Police, he thought.

An initial moment of fear slipped away from his thoughts and Edwin prepared to become the vessel of the All Spirit, a living body inhabited by a god.

Eyes closed, he took in a deep breath, opened his arms wide, and pressed his hands together above his head. A simple squat, performed three times, and he opened his eyes anew, lit by an internal fire.

In his mind, he imagined the All Spirit had taken control of him; the celestial being was inside of his body, forming his fists and directing his thoughts and actions.

I accept you wholeheartedly, he swore.

No traditional exercise had ever appealed to Edwin. Instead, he typically performed a series of hops, flips, and taut-muscle motions that had been mentally provided by the All Spirit to prepare him for hunts and in the event of an outside attack.

164

After years of practice within his home—and now with the All Spirit inside of him—Edwin was sure that he could overtake any foe.

They threaten our cause, the All Spirit moaned within Edwin's mind. *We cannot allow them to thwart our plans. Go, my fledgling. Go...and hunt.*

* * *

Dogs barked from inside the house. There had to be two or three of them. One was a large pit bull that kept appearing in the first floor window.

Shit, she thought. *Move.*

Crouched low, Avery ran into the backyard.

The dogs followed and barked.

A basement door was painted blue. She tried to open it. Locked. There was a porch and a back door. She shuffled up and peeked inside. Instantly, the pit bull's face appeared again. The barking turned ferocious. There were two other dogs, both tiny: a pug and what appeared to be a tea cup poodle. She also spotted numerous cats.

The back door was locked.

She hammered her gun onto one of the glass plates near the lock.

The glass shattered.

The muzzle of the pit bull snapped in the opening. Avery stood up and tracked the movements of all three dogs. When the way was clear, she reached in and unlocked the door.

A squat took her down low. With her back protected by the wooden door, Avery put one hand on the knob. The gun was in her other hand. She listened for the timing: the pit bull barked and jumped, stayed on the floor for a bit, then repeated the process.

When the pit bull was about to jump, Avery opened the door.

The dog rushed out. A light tap with her foot and the pit bull stumbled down the steps. The two other dogs appeared and grasped for footing so they could turn and reach Avery. She simply held the doorknob, spun inside the house, and closed the door.

Barking continued, but it no longer bothered her.

Avery was in.

A cat purred against her leg.

The kitchen was beside her. To her left was a small dining area, and straight ahead were a living room and two more cats. A few

165

plants dotted the kitchen windowsills. They seemed like the easiest variety to maintain: cactus and pothos.

Gun held low, Avery moved through the house.

Stay alert, she thought. He has to know I'm here.

"Edwin Pesh!" she yelled. "This is the police. Make your hands visible and step into view. There are two other officers outside," she lied. "Backup is on the way. In a few minutes, this entire block will be crawling with cops. *Edwin Pesh!*"

Around a corner was the staircase to the second level. More cats lined the steps.

Avery crept up the carpeted stairs, gun pointed straight ahead and above, where she could see a wraparound banister. Cats continued to get in her way. She gently nudged them aside.

The second floor was empty, but she found even more cats. No pictures lined the walls. No photos of any kind. Only two spartan bedrooms that were completely blanketed in cats. Every closet was opened. She looked under beds and in nooks. Edwin Pesh was nowhere.

The basement door was in the kitchen.

Beside the door was a phone.

Avery picked it up and dialed 911.

"This is emergency services," a woman said. "How can I help you?"

"My name is Avery Black. I'm with the Boston A1," she replied and offered her badge number. "I'm in the house of a possible serial killer and need support."

"Thank you for your call, Detective Black. Can you please..."

Avery left the phone hanging.

The basement was dark. A light switch to her right illuminated another door at the bottom of the steps. She made her way down. The walls were lined in bare wood.

At the bottom of the steps, she opened the second door.

Another hallway was perpendicular to the staircase. More dim lights hung from the wooden ceiling and lit the space. She turned left, and was forced to make another quick left into a much longer passageway.

Every square inch of the walls in the longer passage was lined in pictures, hundreds of pictures. The pictures seemed to be arranged horizontally. If she followed one all the way to the right, it told a story. A black cat was in one frame, just sitting on a ledge. In the next frame, the cat was seemingly dead on the ground. In the next, the cat was partially opened to reveal its interior. Each consecutive picture showed the cat in some stage of taxidermy.

Doors interrupted the walls on both sides.

It's like a maze, she thought.

"*Edwin Pesh!*" she yelled. "This is the police. Make yourself known! Put your hands where I can see them and step out into the hall."

She listened for a response.

Nothing, only dogs barking from a distance, and the motion of an orange cat that had followed her down into the basement.

The first door on her left was opened. Darkness obscured the room. Avery clicked on her flashlight, held it in line with her gun muzzle. She spun inside. Jars were visible along the back wall, row after row of jars with multicolored substances. A silver medical table was to her left, along with medical equipment and embalming fluid and tools.

Holy shit.

A cat rubbed against her leg.

Startled by the contact, Avery pointed her weapon down and nearly fired.

"Jesus," she whispered.

For a moment, her eyes closed.

Floorboards creaked behind her. In the second that it took for Avery to rouse herself and spin, she felt a sting in the back of her neck and heard someone run farther down the hall.

Shit!!

Wooziness spread through her.

Not like this, she fought. I can't go out like this.

Energized by the thought that she only had moments before some strange concoction took effect, Avery screamed a muted, barely perceptible howl and stumbled up the hall. She slammed against walls on her way. Pictures flew off and smashed to the floor. Every door she found was opened. The flashlight whipped from one side to the other.

Blindly, she fired.

Images appeared in a dreamy blur: a room that was more like a holding cell with bars and a straw floor; another room full of stuffed cats and dogs.

When she reached the last door, Avery sank to her knees.

The flashlight dropped from her hand.

She turned the doorknob and pushed it open.

167

Edwin Pesh could be seen on the outer edge of the flashlight's glow.

Avery sank to her chest. She held the gun ahead of her and prepared to fire. Suddenly, as light as a feather, Edwin hopped from one side of the room to the other, again and again, in fast, catlike bursts that made him difficult to target.

Woozy. Avery's mind was woozy and fading fast. The gun was heavy, too heavy to hold up. She lowered the weapon to the ground. Her cheek touched the cold floor but she continued to watch Edwin Pesh.

Edwin settled into his low crouch, yellow eyes illuminated from the flashlight.

Avery could feel herself slipping out of consciousness.

Edwin stood to his full height and walked toward her.

"Shhhhh," he whispered.

Not like this, Avery thought.

With great effort—and her wrist balanced on the ground—Avery raised the muzzle of her gun toward Edwin's groin and fired three times. *Crack! Crack! Crack!*

The gun dropped from her hand.

Edwin's feet were in front of her. She could see his legs buckle. Suddenly, he dropped down and sank to the side.

Edwin lay there, collapsed, beside her. His face was but inches away from hers. The two of them lay beside each other, each frozen, each dying, eyes locked on each other's.

His eyes locked on hers. In the dreamy haze of whatever drug had poisoned her system, his eyes appeared incredibly large, wide open pools of darkness. A smile curled on his lips.

"More," he whispered. "*More.*"

Nothing else came out of him, nothing else moved. The lips remained in a partial curl, and his eyes, fully open, burned into her soul.

In her mind, Avery heard, *More. MORE!*

A male voice resounded through the halls.

"Avery!?"

A hand touched her neck and checked for a pulse. Someone cursed and then spoke in a warped, barely recognizable voice: "Talk to me, Black. Can you hear me? Try to stay alive. Help is on the way."

But she felt herself weakening.

His voice came again, this time panic in it.

"Shit, Black, don't die on me now!"

168

CHAPTER THIRTY SIX

Avery awoke in a hospital bed, groggy with a very dry and painful sore throat. Everything in her body ached, as if she'd had all of her blood flushed out and replaced with some kind of heavy, toxic fluid. An IV bag was hooked up to her arm. A heart monitor bleeped from somewhere outside of her view.

The room was filled with balloons and flowers.

On a chair beside her, slumped over in sleep, was Ramirez. He was just as relaxed and perfectly dressed as the first day they'd met. A shiny blue suit adorned his form; the white shirt was bright and highlighted his tan and his slicked-back dark hair.

A nurse walked in.

"You're awake," she noted in surprise.

Avery opened her mouth.

"Don't try to speak just yet," the nurse said. "I'll call the doctor. You must be hungry. Let me see what I can rustle up."

Ramirez roused himself from sleep and yawned.

"Black." He smiled. "Welcome back to the land of the living."

Avery whispered a very painful, scratchy question.

"How?"

"Three days," he said. "You've been out for three days. Oh, man. That was some crazy shit, I can tell you that. You're at Watertown General Hospital. You OK? You want to rest more? Or do you want me to talk?"

Avery never felt so vulnerable in her life. Not only was she laid up in a hospital bed practically unable to move, but she could barely speak.

She nodded and closed her eyes.

"Talk."

"Well, you are one crazy *loca*, Avery Black. At least *somebody* gave you the good sense to call me, and to dial 911 when you were in the house. Now, if you'd waited, maybe you wouldn't be here today. But that's for another time."

"You got him," he said.

The smile came again.

"Three shots, every one of them hit. One in the groin, one through the heart, and the last one in the face. He's dead. No more girls for him.

"You're lucky to be alive." He whistled. "You know that? He pumped you full of some real nasty stuff. Paralyzes the body for

169

about six hours and it slowly eats away at your insides until you die. Doctors had never seen anything like it, but they were able to concoct an antidote based off the syringe he used. Still, it was touch and go there for a while."

She glanced at the flowers and balloons.

"You had a lot of visitors," he said. "Cap came by, Connelly. Even Finley. Wasn't a big deal for them, really. They all followed me to the house."

She gave him a look.

He smirked.

"You might be crazy," he said, "but I'm not. I called Connelly the second you got off the phone with me. *I* needed backup!"

Avery gave him a deep, curious look. His dark brown eyes, typically playful and inquisitive, reached out to her with a warmth and care, as if to offer more.

"You?" she asked.

A blush painted his face red.

"Well," he mumbled and had a difficult time getting the rest out. "I've been here for a while, that's true. Just wanted to make sure my partner was all right. Besides," he shrugged, "I still have to rest up the wound, right? I just thought: why not just do it here? Gets a little lonely sometimes in my apartment, you know? Anyway, I'm glad you're all right," he said and had trouble meeting her gaze. "I'll leave you alone. Doctor keeps saying you need rest."

"No, " she whispered.

Meekly, she reached out her hand.

Ramirez gripped her fingers and held them tight.

CHAPTER THIRTY SEVEN

When word got out that Avery was alive and well, the list of visitors increased. Finley came by in the afternoon, along with Captain O'Malley and Connelly, who waited by the door with his head low.

"Crazy bastard," O'Malley said. "Had a whole garden in that basement of his, on the other side of that medical room. Guy was growing every kind of hallucinogenic plant you can imagine. Had a few contacts lying around too, so we're going to put a stop to that trade route immediately. Great work, Avery."

"Found out about the bodies, too," Connelly chimed in. "He might have worshipped 'The Three Graces' from Roman myth. They were followers of the goddess Venus: three young girls that worshipped beauty. We think maybe that's why he kept them so lifelike in death. Had a bunch of drawings around the house."

Finley kept touching the gifts piled up on the windowsill.

"God damn," he said, "the mayor sent you flowers? I never got nothing from the mayor. I bet if you'd have called *me* for backup, the mayor would have sent *me* flowers, too. Fuckin' Ramirez," he said. "I was your partner. *Me.*"

O'Malley scrunched his face at Avery.

"We'll talk about your lack of protocol when you're ready," he said. "For now, rest up and get better."

* * *

Randy Johnson came to visit Avery later that night. The spunky, short forensics analyst had her hair poofed out into a wild afro. She wore a red polka-dot dress and brought flowers and a newspaper. Avery had just finished her dinner and was already exhausted.

"Hey, girl!" Randy said. "Heard you were up."

Avery attempted a smile.

"Don't try to talk. Don't try to talk," Randy insisted. "I know you've had a busy day already. Just came by to make sure my girl was alive and kicking." Her eyes went wide. "*And gossip!*"

She sat down beside her.

"First of all, I think Dylan Connelly *definitely* has a crush on you. No joke. He came by a few times to check on the case and twice he asked about you. First time was like 'Hey, have you gone

171

to visit Black yet?' Real casual and all. And the second time was today. He was like 'How's Black doing?' I don't think that man has *ever* spoken to me outside of case-related questions. Seriously!? You got yourself a boy toy if you want it."

A disapproving frown lined Avery's face.

"Yeah, he's not for you," Randy said, "but Ramirez? Now he's dreamy. You go and get that boy, girl. He saved your life!"

She smiled, then slowly her smile faded.

"Can we *please* talk about that lady killer?" she added. "Is it too soon?"

Avery gave her the thumbs-up.

"Thirty-six cats," Randy huffed in disbelief. "*Thirty-six!* Who has thirty-six cats? And three dogs? And you want to know what was even crazier than that? They were all female. Not a single male among them. And all those pictures on his wall in the basement? I don't know if you remember that but he had lots of sick pictures of all these cats and dogs and the girls he killed, and each picture showed a different stage of their conversion into stuffed animals, you know? All girls. Crazy white man had a little girls' club all his own. Connelly said it had to do with Roman mythology and Aphrodite and all these women, but I just think the man was nuts."

A sound escaped Avery's lips.

She cleared her throat and focused on a single world.

"Family?"

"Did he have any relatives?" Randy asked to confirm. "Is that what you want to know? Oh, yeah. That guy that shot himself was his uncle. I thought you knew that. It's all here in the paper," she said. "Uncle hired the killer about a year ago. Killer met all those girls at a job fair. Got to know them when they came to the office."

She placed the paper on Avery's chest.

The headline read "College Killer Captured" with a picture of the crime scene. A smaller burst read "Disgraced Attorney Turned Cop in Critical Condition" with an article about how she left a viable crime scene to find the *actual* killer.

"You're a hero!" Randy cheered.

It was hard for Avery to think of herself as a hero or anything else. Her mind was too groggy to focus on anything for very long, and her body remained in a post-paralysis shock that made movement difficult.

Hero. That was not what she wanted. That was never what she'd wanted. She'd just wanted to set wrongs right, to put these bastards away forever.

172

To make amends, she realized, for something for which she would never be able to make amends.

Her eyes grew heavy, and as sleep fell on her, it was hard for her to believe that she'd ever be able to walk again.

CHAPTER THIRTY EIGHT

On Thursday morning, surprisingly, Avery awoke, alert and physically capable. She could easily move her arms without the sluggish weight, sit up on her own, and think clearly. A short conversation with the morning nurse confirmed her throat muscles were stronger.

Events from the house were difficult to recall. She could see the dogs, all the cats, and the strange basement walls made of wood and picture frames. There was even a frightening image of Edwin Pesh like a spider with two glowing eyes, hopping from one side of a room to the other. How she'd gotten out alive? She only remembered a whisper and the face of Ramirez.

The door opened, and Avery looked up in shock. Her heart soared at the sight: Rose came running into the room.

"Mom!" she cried and hugged her tight. "I was so worried about you."

Avery closed her eyes and gripped her daughter just as strongly. Tears fell down her face, as the tight hug warmed her heart.

Avery remembered pieces of their dismal lunch, the message she'd left her before she stupidly entered the house of a killer alone.

She's back, she thought. *My Rose came back to me.*

Rose eventually let her go.

"I've been calling everyone," she said. "I had no idea where you were. No one would give me any answers. *Finally*, your captain called me back and told me you were here and awake. I came as soon as I could."

Avery smiled, hardly able to speak through her tears.

"Mom, I was sick about the way we left things. I'm so sorry. This whole week, all I could think about was: if Mom dies, you'll have to live with the way you acted for the rest of your life. I'm so sorry. It's just…"

Tears ran down Avery's cheek.

"It's *my* fault," she said. "Don't *you* take the blame, Rose. *I'm* the one to blame. I'm your mother, and I promise I'll make this right."

They cried and held hands and in that grip, Avery felt all the heaviness that had been draped around her neck all these years slowly lifting away. This, she realized, was what was restoring her. More than catching any killer could.

They talked and talked, as they had in old times, and didn't release each other's hands for hours. Finally, Avery felt, it was time to live again.

* * *

Ramirez dropped by again around noon. He appeared more relaxed in designer jeans, a light pink button-down T-shirt, and white sneakers.

"Hey, Avery," he said as if he belonged there. "I brought lunch," and he held up a picnic basket. "Hope I'm not too much of a nuisance, but my mother always said the way to a woman's heart is through food."

"You trying to get to my heart?" Avery asked.

"You know, you know," he said without meeting her gaze. "You saved my life. You're my partner. I saved *your* life."

He glanced up.

Dark brown eyes sought out her innermost feelings.

"If you don't want me to stay," he added and opened a basket full of fried chicken and cherries and soda, "I guess I could just go back home."

Avery smiled.

During the difficult times in her life, she'd always sought the company of men like Ramirez. No, she realized. Not *exactly* like him. The other men were harder around the edges, players, more interested in one-night stands than an actual relationship. But Ramirez, she thought, he's sweet. And cute. And he really does seem to care.

He's your partner! her mind blared.

So what? she thought with abandon. This is the *new* you, and the new you can do whatever she wants.

"Stay," she said with a mischievous grin. "I *love* lunch."

175

CHAPTER THIRTY NINE

Avery was released on Friday.

Ramirez picked her up and drove to her car, which was parked a half block away from the killer's house. As they passed, Avery gave it a long, solemn stare.

"You all right?" Ramirez said. "This doesn't freak you out or anything?"

"I'm fine," she replied.

She didn't just feel fine. She felt better than fine.

Everything about her life now seemed different, better. She had plans to see Rose again soon. Ramirez had come by every day to keep her company. The cards she'd received in her hospital room had been humbling. So many people had sent her well wishes that she realized even when she'd *felt* alone in the past three years, she'd never *been* alone.

Avery hopped out and smiled at Ramirez over the hood.

"Well," she said, "this is my stop. Thanks for everything."

"You headed back to the office?"

"Yeah."

"Want me to tag along?"

"Nah," she said. "That's OK. Enjoy your time off. I'm sure I'll have to put you in another life-or-death situation soon."

Ramirez flashed her a winning smile.

"I hope so."

The ride back to the office was extremely emotional for Avery. Excitement and fear swirled through her thoughts. Despite solving the case, she'd stepped over some lines: she had ignored direct orders from her commanding officer and left a crime scene to purse her lead with Edwin Pesh.

It'll be fine, she thought. You got him.

In the police garage, officers gave her purposeful stares and raised their thumbs and fists as she passed.

"Way to go, Black," someone yelled out.

The elevator to the second floor was through the garage itself and inside the ground level of the A1 offices. At the sight of Avery, half the station clapped. Some officers ignored her to do their work, others had blank expressions as if they felt forced to comply with their enthusiastic co-workers, but for the most part, Avery reveled in the moment.

She raised a humble hand, lowered her gaze.

"Thanks."

On the second floor, her reception was even more boisterous. For at least a minute, all work stopped in Homicide so people could stand and clap and nod their heads.

"Serial killers beware!" someone shouted.

"You got him, Black!"

"Good to have you back."

Finley ran up to her, and while he was reluctant to touch or give her too much physical praise in front of the others, he patted her professionally on the back and pointed in her face.

"That's my partner," he said. "You see that? We solve crimes. Fuckin' killers don't stand a chance with the Black and the Finley at her back."

"Back to work." O'Malley clapped from his office door. "Black," he called and waved her forward. "In my office."

Connelly watched her from his desk; gave a curt, grimaced nod to Avery before he turned back to his desk. To Avery, it seemed like he was just shuffling papers around to try and look busy. She kept her eyes on him. After a few seconds—as suspected—he glanced back up. Pissed that he'd been caught, he growled and walked away.

"Close the door," O'Malley said. "Sit down."

Avery closed the door and sat.

"Good to have you back," he said with averted eyes. "How you feeling?"

"I'm better. Thanks."

"As I told you in the hospital, we have a few questions to tie everything up. Let me just go through those first."

He read something off a piece of paper.

"Why did you abandon the crime scene at Villasco's house?"

"He wasn't our guy," she said.

"How could you know that?" he asked and looked at her with curious intent. "The guy shot himself in the head. He worked at Devante. Case closed."

Avery frowned.

"It didn't feel right. He said something, something about family. I can't remember it exactly, but it was like he was covering for someone. No minivan at the house, no room for taxidermy. He seemed lonely, lonely and afraid. It was bugging me, I couldn't let it go, and on the list McGonagle gave me, I had one more lead to check."

"How did Edwin Pesh become a suspect?"

"He lived in Watertown. It made sense that the killer lived in either Watertown or Belmont given the direction of his car from Lederman Park and Cambridge."

"So on a hunch, you abandoned a crime scene, and your partner, and you headed over to Watertown on your own."

"I didn't mean to."

"Hold on," he said. "Not now. First answer the question."

"Correct," she replied.

"What made you call Ramirez? He's out of commission. And 911?"

"As soon as I saw the minivan, I called Dan. I realized I might need help. The 911 call was made in the house. I was getting creeped out by all the animals."

"Why not call Connelly? Or Thompson? Or even Finley. All of them were on your team."

Avery looked up.

"Honestly? I wasn't sure I could trust them."

"So you decided to trust a guy that was recovering from a stab wound? Not a smart move, Avery. It worked out. Ramirez was smart enough to call for backup, but I expect more from someone I just promoted to lead detective. They're your new teammates and you've got to learn how to play well on a team."

When Avery was an attorney, it was every man for himself. Even when she'd been assigned to other lawyers in a research group, everyone was always trying to outdo the other so they could look good in front of the boss. It had been a cutthroat, soulless existence, and that existence had followed her into the A1.

"I can do better," she said.

"Yeah, well, no one's been very welcoming to you since you came upstairs, I get that. And until you personally handled those West Side Killers, you were pretty much persona non gratis downstairs too, right? Things are different now, Avery. You just solved a really big public case."

"Am I back on Homicide?" She asked.

O'Malley raised his brows.

"*'Am I back on Homicide?'* Seriously? You defied my orders to stay away from the case. You left a crime scene. You ignored your partners and nearly got yourself killed. Do you think you *deserve* to be back on Homicide?"

"Yeah," she said with a determined glint in her eyes. "I do."

O'Malley smiled.

"How can I say no to a hero?"

178

He grinned wider.

"Of course you're back!" he said. "Now get out of here. Take the rest of the day off. Come back Monday and start the week fresh. And while you're basking in your current glory, do me a favor?" He ruffled around for a few pieces of paper. "Call the mayor. Here's his personal line. And Miles Standish, too, the owner of Devante. I noticed both of them sent you flowers and a card."

He stood and saluted her, and she was touched by the gesture.

"Great work, Avery."

CHAPTER FORTY

On Saturday morning, Avery purged her apartment.

Boxes of photos were sifted through, along with newspaper articles from the time when she'd defended Howard Randall; clothing she'd worn as an attorney, everything from her past life—a life that no longer defined her. She kept photos of Rose, clothing that had special meaning, but most of it went into the trash.

Lights were turned on—all of them, which she'd never done before—and when she viewed the painted walls and the carpet and kitchen, she thought: you bought this place after Randall and right before you became a cop; it still reeks of your misery from that time. Just like you, this place needs to change.

It's time, she realized, to sell it. To move on. To buy a new place in town, maybe somewhere closer to Rose—if she'd let her.

Avery stood out on her porch and stared at the sky and realized there was still something she had to do, something that would really put an end to the past.

She grabbed her car keys and headed out.

The ride to the South Bay House of Corrections was easy for her now; she'd made the trip so many times. She made a call on the way to reserve an appointment with Howard Randall.

"You can't make appointments on the day of," the woman said.

"This is a big step for me," Avery replied. "I'm *making* an appointment."

"I'm sorry, but we..."

Avery hung up.

At the prison, the guards were quick to congratulate her on finding—and stopping—what had become known as the College Girl Killer. Once again, the female officer inside her green booth was annoyed that Avery hadn't made an appointment, but she recognized her from previous pictures, and now, from the papers.

"You stopped that killer, right?"

"Yeah," Avery said with pride, "I did."

"OK, no appointment needed for you today. Nice work."

Howard Randall had a smile on his face when Avery was led into the conference room in the basement. Hands were cuffed and steepled on the table.

"Congratulations," he said.

"Thanks," Avery replied.

He seemed older than she remembered, and not as powerful. The power he'd had over her life was now, surprisingly, almost gone.

She took a seat.

"I've wanted to say something for a while now," she said. "I've never told this to anyone but, I knew." Her blue eyes gazed deeply into his. "I knew you were guilty when I took your case. Not completely. I mean, you put on a good show but, I had this feeling that everything was about to fall apart because of you."

Randall leaned forward.

Genuine tears glossed his eyes.

"I *know*," he whispered.

"How could you have known?"

"I was caught," Randall said. "There was no denying the connections: they were both students. We'd had lunches and dinners together many times. The murders were presented on campus. One of them had kept a journal. However," he said with a sly smile, "I was certain I could convince a jury of my innocence, a lie detector test, a lawyer, anyone, because you see, Avery, I don't *believe* in your concepts of right and wrong. The murder of those two students was *right* in my mind. It would ultimately help *them*, and the world. Therefore, I was innocent of any wrongdoing, any crime. I was prepared to be set free and to continue my work, only smarter. That is, until I met *you*."

A sigh escaped him.

"What did I see?" he wondered. "A beautiful woman, lost and in desperate need of salvation. You *believed* you were doing right. You *believed* you were doing good, and that belief—that *false* belief—was eating you alive. You couldn't see it, but I could. The only way I knew how…was to show you. To tear down the lie and force you to face the rubble of your life."

"Why?" Avery whispered. "Why me?"

"Isn't it obvious?" Howard said. "I love you, Avery."

The declaration was too much for Avery to handle. She turned away and shook her head.

Love? He destroyed you. Did he? she wondered. Or did he free you from that path you were on? No, she assured herself. He's a killer, a manipulator; no good can come from someone like him. And yet, she was happier now than she'd ever been. The dark gloom that had followed her during her rookie years as a cop had lifted. Her past life as an attorney was now understood for what it had been: a desperate move to escape her former life and be someone she'd never truly enjoyed being in the first place.

Avery stood up to leave.

"Don't go," Howard begged. "*Please*. Not yet."

"What else do you want?"

"You never finished your story," Howard whispered, and a twisted smile formed on his lips, and his eyes were shiny beads.

"My father?" she asked. "You want to know what happened?"

Silently, Howard watched her.

Avery turned away. This part of the story she had never relayed to anyone, not Jack or Rose or the reporters that had interviewed her as a young girl. She remembered her mother's legs in the grass, and the blood on her dress, and her father, standing overhead with the shotgun in his hand.

She took a deep breath, closed her eyes, and prepared to face her deepest demons. She wasn't sure if she was ready.

"I heard them yelling," she began, her voice tremulous.

Then she paused for a good minute before continuing.

"Before the shots," she added. "He was calling her a whore, a worthless, drunken whore, and she was saying vile things to him," she whispered and glanced at Howard for only a moment. "Vile things. Then I heard the shot and saw him there. He laughed, he actually laughed at me, like it was some joke that I'd shown up. He said: 'Go get me a shovel. You have to bury your mother.'"

Avery faced him with tears in her eyes.

"And he made me do it," she said. "I was there until nightfall. I dug that hole all by myself. My arms were shaking, my legs were black with dirt. I honestly thought that whole time that he was going to shoot me and throw me in there with her. I was so scared. Every second felt like an eternity. It was very dark when I was done. No lights anywhere except for the stars. He watched me the entire time. 'Good job,' he said when I was done, and he touched me, he touched me like he'd done before, only this time he was harder, more forceful. I guess now that he'd taken care of my mother, he thought he could finally have his way with *me*."

She looked up and sucked in a deep breath.

"That's when I left," she said. "That very night I ran away from home. Police found me and tried to take me back. I told them, I told them everything. A few months later, I was a ward of the state and assigned to a family. You don't want to know about *that* time," she said. "In some ways, it was worse than with my father."

"I do want to know, Avery," he whispered like a craving alcoholic that only wanted one more drink, "I *do*."

In that moment, Avery saw him for what he truly was: the ugliness, his shriveled features and demonic stare. He reminded her of the story of the butterfly and the cocoon. He was more like the caterpillar in the story, she realized, a slimy, odd creature that was capable of transforming into a beautiful butterfly, but never had.

"You've helped me," she said, with true affection. "In my life, and on the case. I won't be coming back. I don't need to anymore."

Howard leaned back and slowly, demonically, he broke into a grin. But unlike the other times, it was a weak grin, one that showed a crack in his confidence, that showed that he was no longer so sure.

"Oh, you will," he said. "You will."

* * *

Outside the prison the sky was overcast, the first cloudy day in over a week. Since the first day of the case, Avery had longed for rain, longed for clouds to match her mood. Now, she didn't even care.

As Avery walked across the vast parking lot toward her car, she felt lighter than she'd ever had. For the first time in a long time, nothing seemed to matter. In fact, the cooler air and dark clouds felt good: the start of something new.

She stopped and took in the cool breeze, and for the first time in the longest time she felt she had a life ahead of her.

COMING SOON!

Book #2 in the Avery Black mystery series!

Blake Pierce

Blake Pierce is author of the bestselling RILEY PAGE mystery series, which include the mystery suspense thrillers ONCE GONE (book #1), ONCE TAKEN (book #2) and ONCE CRAVED (#3). Blake Pierce is also the author of the MACKENZIE WHITE mystery series.

An avid reader and lifelong fan of the mystery and thriller genres, Blake loves to hear from you, so please feel free to visit www.blakepierceauthor.com to learn more and stay in touch.

Made in the USA
Coppell, TX
20 March 2022

75289572R10111